Isaac Kelso, Richard Hooker Wilmer

The Stars and Bars

The Reign of Terror in Missouri

Isaac Kelso, Richard Hooker Wilmer

The Stars and Bars
The Reign of Terror in Missouri

ISBN/EAN: 9783337409081

Printed in Europe, USA, Canada, Australia, Japan

Cover: Foto ©Andreas Hilbeck / pixelio.de

More available books at **www.hansebooks.com**

THE

STARS AND BARS;

OR,

THE REIGN OF TERROR IN MISSOURI.

BY

ISAAC KELSO,

OF PLATTE CITY, MO.

Sail on, O Union, strong and great:
Humanity, with all its fears,
With all its hopes of future years,
Is hanging breathless on thy fate.

To the

Gallant Soldiers of our Loyal Army,

who,

in the Defence of the Government, and for the Preservation of

OUR GLORIOUS UNION,

have bravely followed the Stars and Stripes over ensanguined

plains and through storms of iron hail,

and

To the self-sacrificing Patriots of the land everywhere,

This Work is most respectfully Dedicated by

THE AUTHOR.

PREFACE.

THE first draft of what is here offered to the reading public was sketched amid the whirlwinds of civil war, and while encompassed by the most exciting scenes and circumstances of violence, conspiracies, and sanguinary strife. It claims to be, for the most part, but a plain, unvarnished story of what happened under the author's own observation, during a reign of terror which has scarcely had a parallel in the history of our race.

It is hoped the courteous reader will not mistake the production for a work of imagination; the author is free to admit, however, that, in some cases, he has used fictitious names; and, also, that the conversations, dialogues, and soliloquies introduced more or less throughout the work are, in part at least, supposed. But no further than this has he used the guise of fiction, or essayed to idealize his subject; for we have come upon times when, of a truth, it may be said that "fact is stranger than fiction." For the marvellous, the wild, the thrilling, we no longer need to draw upon fancy; reality, now, exceeds the most highly-wrought creations of imagination, transcends the most startling coinage of the brain.

While the author has been solicitous to paint vividly and lifelike, yet he must insist that his picture is by no means overdrawn, or highly colored. The incidents related, the events and characters brought forward, are *real*, and intended, without contributing aught to prejudice and passion, to make a fair and truthful impression on the candid mind.

Should there be found, here and there, a passage that savors of acrimony, or betrays a spirit of vindictiveness, the indulgent reader will please bear in mind that the writer has had an interior view of the rebellion, and passed through an ordeal well calculated to set any frail mortal's blood on fire. For, from the beginning of the trouble, and long before the Federal Government had given the slightest protection to loyal citizens anywhere in the Southwest, he was constantly surrounded by lawless men, plotting traitors, and assassins, who, like bloodhounds, were ready to hunt down, rob, or murder, their patriotic neighbors.

Regarding the present conflict as a death-struggle between civilization and barbarism, liberty and slavery, loyalty and treason; and convinced that the great body of the Northern people have no adequate conception of the actual state of things at the South; and persuaded, also, that there is an apathy at the North, from which patriots need to be awakened at such a time of peril to the country, it is deemed at least pertinent to hold the mirror up to reality, and lift the curtain behind which the most shocking tragedies have been enacted, and in the shadow of which disloyal men still skulk and traitors hide themselves.

The humble volume here respectfully submitted to the public is designed, without ostentation or pretension, to put a candle in every honest man's hand who needs more light on a subject confessedly of absorbing interest to us all.   I. K.

THE STARS AND BARS.

CHAPTER I.

IT was in the hill-country of North-western Arkansas, and in the spring of 1861. Twilight was deepening into darkness. The loud shout of the guerrilla chief to his scattered band, and the distant clatter of iron hoofs upon the rocky hill, had just died away on the dusky air. Adrian Malvin, a youth of scarce eighteen summers, odious in the eyes of disloyal men and traitors on account of his unswerving adherence to the cause of the Union, and hunted like a wolf from forest to plain, from hill-top to valley, stood trembling in a gloomy dell, where he had sought shelter from the red-handed vandals who clamored for his blood.

Though hard pressed in his flight, he had managed to elude pursuit amid the mazes of the rooky wood and tangled copse into which he had plunged.

The baffled banditti, despairing of accomplishing their diabolical purpose and murderous designs, had abandoned the chase, leaving the persecuted patriot to the quietude of the lonely forest and the solemn darkness of the night.

Malvin was a young man of limited experience, — knew but little of the world, and almost nothing of life's trials, buffets, and conflicts, and still less of the treachery, baseness, and brutality which lurk in the hearts of bad men.

Although reared in the midst of a community made up, for the most part, of the baser sort, he had no conception of the terrible depravity of men whose consciences were seared, and whose lives were wholly given up to crime.

Surroundings and associations, doubtless, have much to do in forming the characters of men;

yet men are not all the same under the same circumstances. The influences of society, of scenery, and of example, brought to bear on the human mind and heart, though potent, are by no means omnipotent.

Malvin had been taught that slavery was a divine institution, and that the colored race had no rights which a white man was bound to respect; yet his own heart told him that oppression was a crime. Vice in every form prevailed around him, and scenes of cruelty and injustice were constantly before his eyes; yet he maintained an upright walk and spotless reputation, and unfolded his faculties, moral and intellectual, in rare harmony, beauty, and purity.

Unsophisticated, guileless, and open-hearted, he was ever frank in the expression of his opinions, and hesitated not, on any subject, to state his honest convictions; and when the madness of secession came up, he stopped not to consider consequences or to count the cost, but with all the zeal and energy of his ardent soul opposed and denounced it. He had yet to learn that all were not men that wore the human form. It is hard for a generous mind to believe others treacherous. Malvin was unsuspecting; nor would he admit that men could be so base, till the unwelcome conviction forced itself upon him. Soon as the work of rebellion began, he found to his cost that the tiger was unchained; and that multitudes he had been accustomed to look upon as men were being transformed, as by magic, into demons.

A new phase of depraved human nature, to his great surprise, now met his gaze, filling his heart with unutterable sadness, and causing wild, strange thoughts to sweep across his bewildered brain.

"Oh, God!" exclaimed he, in the bitter anguish of his soul, "has it come to this, — that loyalty is reckoned a crime? — and that an American citizen, for his political opinions, is thus persecuted, driven from his home, and hunted like a wild beast? Alas, that I have lived to see this evil day!"

The eruption, the worse than volcanic eruption, which began with such violence, betokened the speedy overthrow of all law and order, —

the breaking up of society, and utter ruin to the country! What a shadow fell upon young Malvin's heart and hopes!

As Night gathered her sable curtains more closely about him, he gave his mind to sad reflections upon his forlorn condition and the fiendish persecution he was suffering. In the midst of his melancholy meditations, he was startled all at once by a gang of wolves, that, from the depths of the dark forest, set up a doleful howling.

"Welcome!" cried Malvin, after a moment's reflection, "thrice welcome, ye wild beasts of prey, whose nature it is to howl and prowl. I hail you as companions and friends, in preference to my fellow-men! Welcome to this dreary wild! where, alike, we woo the darkness and the gloom, to find refuge from the cruelty of human beasts and hellish monsters in the shape of men!"

Now, from a neighboring tree, hard by, a hooting owl joined in the dismal chorus, as if to make the grim night and lonely glen still more hideous.

"And welcome to the voice of the night-owl!" said Malvin; "thy harshest note is music to my ear, compared to the horrid oaths, the taunts and gibes, the profane and vulgar jests, of the cut-throat clans that infest this God-forsaken land!"

It may be here remarked, that the conduct of the desperadoes in the Southwest, who were then plundering the country, maltreating peaceable citizens, and murdering loyal men, was the more unpardonable and outrageous, inasmuch as there had yet been no invasion from the North of which to complain. Nor had the Federal Government, up to that period, taken a single step toward sending an armed force into the country.

It is a noteworthy fact, by the way, that the most appalling scenes enacted, and the most revolting pictures of violence and bloodshed, which the eyes of men have looked upon since the inauguration of civil war in our unhappy country, transpired, strange as it may seem, before there were any organized armies in the field on either side.

It may be further stated, in this connection, and in strict fidelity to truth, that before the present administration came into power, even prior to the presidential election, and on the day of the election, many a poor German was murdered in cold blood, by the brutal mob, for his political predilections and anti-slavery proclivities; and the civil authorities and officers of the law connived at it. In this villany, the complicity of the pro-slavery *clergy* should not be overlooked, especially the clergy of the Methodist Church, South. These Reverend traitors did more than any other class of men to encourage intolerance, foster a mobocratic spirit, and bring about a recklessness, the legitimate fruits of which were to barbarize the community, and turn loose upon the country hordes of robbers, incendiaries, and assassins! For the credit of religion, this disgrace might be left unrecorded, did not patriotism and the exigency of the times require that disloyal men should everywhere be *marked*, — especially at such a time of peril as this, when we are in the midst of the most fearful revolution that ever black-ened the political heavens of any nation. Than the clergy, no recreant wretches in Rebeldom have been more rabid, lawless, and blood-thirsty. The preachers of Arkansas and Missouri, with here and there a rare exception, were regular fire-eaters; they out-heroded Herod, and left in the shade even the loud-mouthed demagogue, the black-hearted kidnappers, and soulless slave-traders. Yes; astounding as it may seem, and disgraceful as it must appear, incumbents of the pulpit lent themselves to the cause of secession and treason in the most unscrupulous and reckless manner; sanctioned the murder of political heretics, as Union men were esteemed; apologized for perjury, in disregarding the oath of allegiance; and justified all the diabolical barbarism of the guerrilla system, which caused a reign of terror, throughout the Southwest, that has had no parallel in the history of nations, — no; not even in the worst days of the French Revolution. .

But to return to our youthful hero. Malvin, before the breaking out of the rebellion, had some time marked with serious apprehensions the portentous aspect of the political sky, and watched with anxiety the coming of the gray shadow of secession, and the constant deepening of the gloom; yet he little dreamed that the black cloud of civil war was destined so soon to blot the sun, and from its fretted bosom hurl the thunderbolts of death. Although he quailed in the beginning of the reign of terror, and fled in dismay when, with the resistless power of the whirlwind, the storm first broke upon his own head; yet it will be seen that the fiery ordeal, through which he was called to pass, directly drew out the strong points of his character, developed indomitable energy, fired his soul with dauntless courage, and transformed him into a hero.

Such is the tendency of adversity and trying scenes upon sterling natures. Calamity, suffering, and persecution become the crucible in which the precious metal of the soul is separated from the dross. In Malvin, it at once brought out the pure gold of manly virtue and true patriotism. And, by the way, a

thought is here suggested on which it may not
be unprofitable to expatiate a moment. It is
this: While the terrible civil war, now upon us,
has brought, and is daily bringing, direst calamities and untold sorrows, yet at the same
time it has, with its numberless ills and long
train of evils, brought also no little good; and
is certainly destined, in the end, to work out
great and glorious results.

Not least among the benefits already realized
are the testing of principle in men and the de-
velopment and unveiling of their true characters.

Never before, in this world's history, has there
been such an opportunity for men to show themselves, and to make known the stuff they are
made of.

Under the pressure and white heat of excitement, consequent upon such times, the moral
complexion of the soul, the real principles of
men, and their inherent qualities of mind and
heart, be they what they may, are necessarily
brought out in a strong light. The tossing of
the waves, the surging of the sea, when the

tempest flaps her dark wings, discover the coral reefs, or lay bare the black rocks below the surface; so the gusts of passion, in stormy times like these, the gales that sweep over the mind, and the crowding on of great and stirring events, strip all actors in the scene of their outward guise, and we see men as they are, read their hearts, discern their secret motives, and comprehend their actions.

Since the beginning of our unhappy and most sanguinary struggle, how many men, who, in the "piping times of peace," put on blandishments, gracious smiles, and fairest external seeming, have turned out treacherous, selfish, unprincipled, and hollow-hearted! And how many of great pretensions, of lofty airs, wonderful parade, pomp, and show, have proved themselves but chaff,— made up of vanity, and lighter than a puff of empty air!

At the same time, how many in the humbler walks of life, unpretentious, simple-hearted, and of plain, homely exterior, after passing through the fire, have come out pure and sparkling diamonds of the first water!

2*

The mighty commotion, upheavals, and convulsions, of the country have so sifted men North and South, East and West, that we begin to see what material they are composed of, and to understand their real characters. While the caldron has been boiling, they have found their affinities, and unconsciously ranged themselves where they belong.

True patriots and self-sacrificing citizens, who have been the salvation of the country, loom up like stately columns of pure, white marble, dotting and adorning our fair land, while traitors are everywhere covered with shame and disgrace; and the vile copperhead, with his brains out, and swollen with venom, lies helpless in his snaky folds, a miserable spectacle in the eyes of all honest men, and abhorred alike by Heaven and earth!

Men who have stood by their country in its peril, in its struggle, in its agony, have won a name that will live after them,—a renown more durable than marble, and a glory fadeless as the stars that gem the sky; but the memory of traitors shall be left to rot.

Malvin passed the night in the dreary wild, meditating, with burning brain and agony of thought, through the weary, sleepless hours, upon the hapless events of the preceding day; and speculating, with vague conjecture, upon the future, which seemed, to his inexperienced mind, impenetrably dark, and full of painful uncertainty. The surrounding gloom and oppressive loneliness of the place, doubtless, had something to do in depressing his spirits and filling his mind with trooping phantoms and horrible forebodings. Outward darkness, unquestionably, has great influence over our thoughts and feelings, imparting its own sable complexion thereto.

With the dawn of day, light fell upon the young man's mind as well as upon his outward vision. While the mantle of night disappeared before the radiant eye of the rising morn, the cloud of despondency lifted from the patriot's heart. Everything like fear and trembling at once departed, and he straightway resolved to return to his home, arm himself, defend his person and property as best he could, and stand by the *old stars and stripes* to the last.

CHAPTER II.

"Oh for a world in principle as chaste
As this is gross and selfish!"

———

ALAS, what pains poor mortals take to make life wretched, and turn this beautiful world into a hell!"

Thus soliloquized Parson Southdown, as he leisurely strolled, one bright spring morning, along the margin of a beautiful prairie in the vicinity of Platte City, Missouri.

In his tones there was a shade of sadness, and in his look a touch of melancholy. He walked on, sweeping his restless eye over the verdant landscape, as one who sought to tranquillize a perplexed and troubled mind.

"The golden sun climbs the sky," continued he, "to behold the green-robed earth rejoicing in her queenly attire. How radiant the face of nature! And how sweet is the breath of spring! But oh, how can the sun continue to shine, how can creation smile, and the gentle breezes whisper peace, as with perfumed wings they fan my feverish brow, while fire and sword are doing their fearful work, while bloody murder stalks forth with stained hands and reeking blade, and rapine and violence desolate the land!"

He paused, and pressed his throbbing temples, sighed, and uttered a word of prayer; then, lifting his eyes to the blue sky, said, "The heavens look down as serenely, and all nature is as tranquil, as though no stormy passions raged in the human breast. The birds sing as merrily, and hill and dale bloom as gayly, as if men were happy, and cherished toward one another no enmity. Even these new-born, dewy flowers are smiling through their tears. And how gently come the yellow beams of the morning sun to kiss away those glistening, pearly tears! Oh that the angel of love would, in like manner, come to kiss away the burning drops of grief that to-day dim the eyes of thousands in this distracted land!"

Now, leaning upon his staff, he stood for some moments silent and motionless, as if lost in profound and gloomy reflection ; then, suddenly looking up, and starting forward, as if just waking from a painful dream, he said to himself, "Is there not a God of justice ?   Why should so wicked a people marvel at his judgments ? "

A familiar voice, at this juncture, called out to him, "Good-morning, parson ! "   And the next moment a horseman was by his side, whom he greeted as Clifton Clifford.

" You walk at an early hour, Mr. Southdown," remarked the latter.

" I like the fresh, balmy air that breathes over these green prairies and blooming lawns," replied the parson ; " and I love to gaze," continued he, " on those wide, bright plains when yon shining orb pours his earliest light upon their emerald bosoms.   Besides, I delight in the unbroken quiet which reigns here before the bustling world's astir."

" Ah, we shall all sigh for quietude, I apprehend," returned Clifford, " ere our country's troubles have an end."

" Indeed, we may," said the parson. " Any news since our last mail ? "

" Many rumors are on the wing; the most reliable of any importance is from a traveller at the inn, who reports the bombardment of Fort Sumter by the rebels."

" Can that be so ? "

" From the tenor of the report, it is likely to be true. And the electric wires, 'tis said, are everywhere burdened with the news."

" Then has already begun the opening act of the most fearful tragedy the world has ever seen."

" If Major Anderson and his little band should be compelled to surrender, alas for our poor country! And that event must surely happen; for the enemy, it seems, is pouring shot and shell upon them at a furious rate."

" And make they no resistance ? "

" Oh, yes. At last accounts, they were returning the fire in the most spirited manner. Gun was answering gun, while sea and shore shook to the fierce reverberations of their terrible thunder."

"I sadly fear the effect of this news on our own population."

"Doubtless it will add fuel to the fire already kindled."

"Yes, and tend to encourage the lawless miscreants of Border-ruffiandom in the fiendish work already begun. Vile men and heartless wretches, of whom Western Missouri is full, will seize upon the event as a suitable pretext for a new and more desperate outbreak. The wild excitement, which has been sweeping like a tempest over the Gulf States, will not be long reaching Missouri. And here it may rage, with even more violence than there."

"What the end will be, God only knows!" observed Clifford; and, bidding the parson good-morning, spurred his steed, and galloped away across the prairie.

"A deep darkness wraps the future," said the clergyman to himself; and, turning about, directed his steps homeward.

In the evening of the same day on which occurred the above conversation, there might have

been seen, in the back-parlor of an elegant mansion, situated in the suburbs of Platte City,
three well-dressed, middle-aged men, sitting near
together in a semicircle, and earnestly engaged
in close conversation.

"Great times make great men," remarked one
of the trio, in a suppressed, yet emphatic, voice.
"We must not let slip the golden ball of opportunity," added he; "what say you, Macqueen?"

"I am growing less sanguine," responded the
individual addressed. "Our plans have, so far,
turned out miserable failures."

"And are you about to recant?"

"That is, perhaps, too late. But if it were
within my power to recall the past, I would take
not another step on the fearful path of secession. We vainly hoped the revolution would be
bloodless; but that silly delusion has already
been dispelled from our minds."

"Nonsense!" impatiently replied the other;
"blood will fatten the soil, let it flow. But we'll
be careful of our own."

"When sanguinary revolutions begin, there's
no telling where they'll end."

" Too irresolute, — want the nerve, I take it."

" I must confess, Ryan, that I've no thirst for blood, but a great horror of human slaughter. Already have we had enough of it."

" What has so changed your purpose? In the beginning, you were resolute, determined, and ready to hazard everything in the cause of secession, and even willing to sacrifice your best friends rather than fail."

" I was then drunk on vain hopes and a mad ambition, but recent events have made me sober and sick at heart. 'Twas but yesterday, my nearest neighbor, a good and valuable citizen, was assassinated, — shot like a dog! and by a member of our Order!"

" His death was decreed by the Castle, and the honorable Knight who put a bullet in his brain was, by high authority, appointed his executioner."

" All the worse."

" How dare you say so? You are a member of the Order, and belong to the Inner Temple of the Knights of the Golden Circle."

" Say, rather, Knights of the Bloody Circle,—

since we have become a band of assassins, whose chief business it is to murder our political enemies."

"Have you so soon forgotten your oath?"

"No. I but too well remember it. God forgive me that I have kept it so well."

"You have a sickly conscience; it needs physic."

"So it does; a medicine that can take away the stains of blood."

"This squeamishness comes of your *higher-law* proclivities. I have sometimes observed that these *higher-law men*, all have tender-footed, weak-kneed consciences."

"Is there no danger of eavesdroppers here?" inquired the third individual, who, up to this time had kept silent. "If I mistake not," added he, "I've thrice seen a shadow pass the window. It looked like the figure of a woman, closely hooded and mantled."

"A servant, perhaps," said Macqueen; "it can be no one else. My wife is from home, — gone to spend the night with a neighbor in the country. Had she not been absent, we should have met elsewhere."

"And is she opposed to secession?" asked Ryan, with surprise.

"Uncompromisingly," replied Macqueen in a low voice; "let us talk softly," he added; "walls have been known to have ears. Our room being dark, no one can see us from without. And none of the servants, I'm sure, saw us when we came in. Some of them may be idly passing about, but will not likely overhear us."

"Then, resuming the subject," remarked Ryan, "let us come at once to the point. This attack on Fort Sumter will no little favor our designs by fanning the flame of excitement, which is preparing the pro-slavery part of the community, in this section, to make a clean sweep of the Dutch and abolition Missourians. We can do anything, you know, with the white trash when once we get them properly excited. They'd run their heads full-tilt against a stone wall if we were but to tell them to. The poor devils want no higher honor than to be our tools. And they hate abolitionists a great sight worse than we do. For they know, if the niggers get free, they'll soon have competition for menial employment. So you see, as we've got to use these ragamuffins in putting down Union men, it's expedient that we lay hold of every event calculated to inflame their passions."

"And what do you propose to do with our Union neighbors?"

"Every mother's son among them has got to do one of three things, — renounce their Union doctrine, leave the country, or swing upon a halter. Between these three things they will be forced to choose."

"That is madness."

"He is a madman who calls it madness."

"These Union men have the same right to the country we have, and the same right to their opinions that we have to ours. Their homes are sacred; their families are dear to them, and rightfully look to them for protection. We have no more right to molest them than they have to molest us."

"If that kind of doctrine is to be preached, we may as well abandon the cause at once; the whole scheme falls to the ground; secession is a failure, and we have our trouble for our pains.

3*

According to our oath and obligation, as Knights of the Golden Circle, we are bound to go forward at all hazards, and at whatever cost, in achieving the independence of the Slave States. To accomplish our purpose, we are bound to stop at nothing. No man's life is to be a stumbling-block in the way of ultimate success. And, as Knights of the *Inner Temple*, we are pledged to take Missouri out of the Union or take her to perdition."

" To do the latter may be found easier than the former."

" Have you no ambition ? "

" Too much, alas'! unless it were of a better quality. Ambition burns like fire in my bones, and, to gratify it, I am ready to do almost anything but commit murder."

" A man of ambition can never have a better opportunity than the present. If secession shall accomplish its mission, a thing most certain, each State, in the end, will likely set up for itself, and choose its own form of government. As to Missouri, we contemplate nothing short of an empire, — an empire, of which *slavery* is to be the chief corner-stone. When that happens, then will be our chance to climb."

"That is all very fine; but there's no use deceiving ourselves, and building castles in the air. The revolution may indeed succeed, and you and I may gain seats of power, but only through blood."

"There's Banquo's ghost again, — blood! blood! You can't endure the thought of blood."

"I confess the weakness."

"Then talk not of ambition; dream not of reaching dizzy heights in this world. No man need hope to grasp a sceptre, wear purple robes, or place a crown upon his brow, till he can say to Conscience and pale-faced Fear, — Avaunt!"

While this conversation was going on, a slight click in the lock of the outer door might have been heard by an acute listener; directly after which, the door softly opened, and in glided a female figure, with the stealthy movement of a ghost. Gently closing the door behind her, she passed cautiously across the floor to the opposite side of the drawing-room, and, bending her ear close to the great folding-doors, which separated the front from the back parlor, stood for some moments in a listening attitude ; then, gliding back to the centre of the apartment, lit a great silver chandelier which hung suspended from the ceiling. In a moment, the room was brilliantly illuminated. But the occupants of the adjoining apartment, who were sitting in profound darkness, perceived it not. For in the folding doors there was not even so much as a keyhole to admit a single stray beam.

Now the mysterious shadow that had thrice passed the window of the conspirators turned out a veritable woman ; and, throwing off her disguise, she stood forth the proud mistress of the mansion.

But the gentle, sunny smile she was wont to wear had disappeared ; her sweet expression was gone ; and her ruby lips, turning ashy white, pressed tightly against her firm-set teeth, her bosom heaved with violent emotion, and her large, lustrous eyes flashed fire.

After a pause, as if to regain self-possession,

she tiptoed to the folding-doors, and, slyly removing a fastening, gave them a vigorous and sudden shove, at the same time gliding back underneath the flaring chandelier.

The folding-doors parting in the centre, each wing swung back upon its hinges, allowing a sudden flood of dazzling light to be poured into the faces of the conspirators.

Never were men more astonished, nor worse confounded. If a thunderbolt had fallen through the roof, or the earth yawned beneath their feet, they could not have manifested more surprise.

On recovering a little from the effect of the first burst of light upon their overpowered vision, they were greatly abashed and confused by the withering, petrifying glance of the majestic woman who stood before them like an avenging angel.

Never did an indignant woman assume an attitude more haughty and commanding. Tall of stature, beautiful in figure, handsome of feature, and fired as was her soul with intense excitement, she looked august and terrific as an angry goddess.

After hurling upon the plotting trio, for a moment, the fierce lightning of her eye, she strode proudly across the chamber, mingling a look of ineffable scorn with an air of lofty disdain and bitter indignation; then, turning about, again bent her eagle gaze upon the dumfounded traitors, especially on him whose treason touched her deepest, — her husband, — and said : —

"Has it come to this, — our house the resort of rebels?"

"Rebels! Rebels!" echoed the disloyal associates of her husband, exchanging sharp glances, and putting on an air of insulted dignity.

"And you, Mr. Macqueen, their boon companion!" continued the indignant woman. "Such being your affinities, the same roof cannot much longer shelter us."

"Madam, what mean you?" demanded the trembling husband, rising to his feet, and making an awkward, but desperate, effort to put on an air of authority.

"My words are plain," answered she, with a

peculiar stress of voice, and again strode haughtily across the apartment.

"In Heaven's name, consider what you say," rejoined Macqueen; "insult not these gentlemen."

"Drive them hence!" said she, with startling emphasis and sweeping gesture.

"This is disgraceful!" muttered the confused husband, with downcast look and faltering voice.

"Disgraceful? Ay, so it is, — having made your house a den of thieves! Away! all of you, away!"

"Let us withdraw," whispered Ryan to his companion; "she's bent on raising Beëlzebub."

"Agreed!" gasped the other; "lead the way; let · us vanish before we're annihilated. I wouldn't be her husband for a kingdom."

Saying which, they slid out at a back-door, and quickly disappeared in the darkness of the night.

There was now silence for a space, save the emphatic footfall of Mrs. Macqueen, who continued to walk up and down the apartment, as if nursing her indignation to keep it warm.

Meanwhile, her husband stood in a sulky mood, dejected and speechless, looking like a criminal at the bar of justice.

"I've no patience," at length said she, "with the black-hearted knaves engaged in this foul conspiracy."

"Am I no longer master of my own house?" stammered Macqueen, seeming at a loss what to say for himself, yet compelled to say something.

"The willing slave of Satan, and the abettor of secession," replied she, in a tone of defiance, "shall not be my master."

"The viper's tongue hath a deadly poison," returned he, with half-averted face, and in a hissing, bitter voice.

"If with mine I could slay vile men and traitors," quickly answered she, "then might I hope to serve my country, and rid the world of wretches not worthy to live in it."

"And can such malice nestle in a heart that's wont to be so gentle?" said Macqueen, half aside and half audibly, while he walked to the opposite side of the chamber, manifestly much overcome with emotion. After a short silence, he turned to his wife and feelingly said, " For years, Florence, we've together lived and loved, while not an unkind word ever passed thy lips or mine to mar our peace."

" Yes, yes; for, until now, you were true to your wife and loyal to your country; but you have at length, and at once, proved false to the one and a traitor to the other."

" A traitor! Do you say traitor?" cried he, with sudden passion and in terrific accents; at the same time wheeling round, and dashing from one side of the house to the other like a maniac.

" Ay, traitor!" she repeated with emphasis. " What else should I call the man who plots in secret the downfall of the government that protects him, and to which he owes everything he counts dear?"

" You wrong me."

" No; I've rightly named you, — traitor."

" You wrong me, Florence," he repeated in a faltering voice, the tremulous and melancholy intonations of which betrayed a deep-felt anguish of mind.

"How can I wrong the man who associates himself with vile conspirators, heartless assassins, and cold-blooded murderers? If these men, themselves, do not rob and kill, they encourage the cut-throats who do. Wrong you? Had I the poison of asps under my tongue, and were my words barbed arrows, dipped in the venom of perdition, I could not wrong such a man."

"But hear me!"

"Go on."

"If I seek to destroy the Union, 'tis only that I might see erected upon its ruins a great Southern Empire."

"Oh, I dare say! Or rather, perhaps, an oligarchy, wherein the rich might lord it over the poor. Mark my words; you are about to leap from a precipice,—a steep and frightful precipice."

"Groundless apprehensions! you torment yourself to no purpose." Saying which, he withdrew from the apartment, leaving his wife in tears.

CHAPTER III.

"There is some soul of goodness in things evil,
Would men observingly distil it out."

AN obscure village in North-western Arkansas, or, more properly, Arkansaw, was the birth-place of Adrian Malvin, the youthful patriot introduced in the beginning of our story.

The veritable Arkansaw traveller, of whom everybody has heard, out of derision, while temporarily sojourning there, called the place, Scallawagville; which name it has never been able to shake off, and by which it is now more widely known than by any other. Its inhabitants, for the most part, are made up of a rude, dissipated, and lawless class of people; yet some progress has been made, on the part of missionaries, in civilizing and Christianizing the population.

The most successful and indefatigable among the heralds of the cross at Scallawagville, up to the breaking out of the rebellion, was Rev. Dr. Elmore, a native of Old Virginia. For many long years this gospel veteran had labored there to build up religion, morality, and virtue among the people. A goodly number, through his instrumentality, had been led to the cross, and became valuable members of society. But the multitude remained hard, impenitent, and reckless. To all intents and purposes they were barbarians, — unthinking, unfeeling barbarians and reprobates, scarcely more civilized than the wild Indians that roam over the plains and through the forests.

The savage disposition. of a portion of the population displayed itself in the most shocking manner, a few years ago, in their treatment of a Yankee book-pedler, against whom, without any just cause or provocation, they had become enraged. The circumstance is almost too horrible to record; yet it may serve to show us how deeply depraved bad men are capable of becoming when they surrender themselves to passion and prejudice.

The crime of which the poor book-pedler was accused and found guilty was that of having three copies of "*Uncle Tom's Cabin,*" among his stock. A mob of three or four hundred men took the unfortunate man a mile or two out of the village, chained him to his wagon, and burned him to death by a fire made chiefly of his own books.

In vain did the victim of their cruelty plead that these obnoxious books were not intended for their slaves, — whom they all knew could not read, — but for free white men. With insults, cursing, and savage yells, they drowned his voice till he perished amid the devouring flames.

When the present rebellion came up, such heartless wretches as these were of course ready to play a conspicuous part, and to enact deeds of fiendish cruelty. Their conduct in the beginning of the rebellion is dimly shadowed forth in the following sketch:—

It was Sabbath morning. The church-bells of Scallawagville were ringing loud and clear. Saints and sinners filled the streets, and all seemed hurrying on in one direction, — evidently drawn by some exciting cause to one common point of attraction.

It had been whispered about, during the preceding week, that Parson Elmore, the pastor of the principal church in the village, and the only loyal minister, perhaps, in all Arkansas, was to be mobbed the next attempt he made to preach a Union sermon. The rumor had created no little sensation; and, as the Sabbath drew on, the excitement increased, and at length had become intense.

At an early hour, the meeting-house, a spacious building, was densely packed; while the other places of worship were almost entirely deserted, — everybody being eager to witness the expected riot. Scores of ruffians, blacklegs, rumsellers, and loafers, who rarely ever had seen the inside of a church, were on hand, ready and anxious to take a hand in mobbing the minister. The crowd awaited with great impatience the arrival of the obnoxious preacher. By and by, a venerable-looking man, with snowy locks, solemn countenance, and thoughtful expression, made his appearance, leaning upon his staff, and slowly wending his way to the house of God. His air was calm, meek, and gentle; yet there was something of sorrow and sadness mingled with the heavenly radiance that beamed from his eye and lit up his intelligent face.

The venerable pastor was met at the threshold by a committee, who informed him that he would not be allowed to preach unless he agreed to renounce his political opinions, give up his Union sentiments, and publicly apologize for what he had said in the pulpit against secession the previous Sabbath.

"Would you have me so dishonor my gray hairs?" replied the hoary-headed minister. "In my youth, and through my manhood's prime," continued he, "I have loved my country, and been proud to prove myself a patriot; and think you, I can now consent, in the evening of my days, and while my head is blossoming for the grave, to become a traitor? Heaven forbid!"

The committee, not entirely lost to all sense of shame, seemed much confused, and, after some hesitancy, proposed that the services might proceed, on condition that nothing be said from the pulpit against secession, nor in favor of the Union. To this the minister made no answer, but, turning about, pressed his way along the crowded aisle to the pulpit.

A murmur of dissatisfaction was now heard among the rabble who hung round the doors and filled the windows and aisles. And rebel professors, as well as disloyal worldlings, muttered, gnashed their teeth, and looked daggers.

Adrian Malvin, with a few reliable friends by his side, had planted himself near the pulpit, and stood with his right hand upon his revolver, resolved, at all hazards, to defend his loyal pastor, ay, even if it cost him the last drop of blood in his veins.

Calmly, and apparently with the utmost composure, the man of God commenced the solemn services of the sanctuary.

After reading an impressive Scripture lesson, he offered up a most fervent and patriotic prayer to the great Ruler of the universe, in behalf of the country, and for the upholding of the government and the preservation of the Union.

A gang of turbulent fellows, near the door, had the indecency to hiss and groan several times during the prayer.

Soon as the minister closed his address to the throne of grace, three stalwart ruffians came rudely pushing their way down the aisle, swearing vengeance against the Union preacher, and evidently bent on violence.

As they neared the pulpit, they were unexpectedly confronted by Malvin, who, drawing his pistol, assured the foremost man that another step would cost him his life.

The villains halted; for they plainly saw in Malvin's eye unfaltering courage, deep earnestness, and cool determination.

In vain did the brutal herd on the outskirts of the congregation urge them forward; the courage of the bullies had oozed out; nor could all the goading and spurring of the mob rally it again.

The minister now began, kindly and mildly, to expostulate with the turbulent and disorderly part of the multitude; but his voice was directly drowned by the hootings and howlings of the rabble.

"Order! order!" cried a respectable citizen in the midst of the assembly. "Let us have some respect, at least, for gray hairs, and not forget that this venerable minister has preached to us twenty years. Besides, no man should be condemned unheard."

But still the rabble continued yelling, hooting, and howling, and calling the man of God everything they considered reproachful, — a black republican, abolitionist, a devil, &c.

. "Bear in mind," said the citizen, again raising his voice above the tumult, "that Parson Elmore is not a foreigner; neither is he a Yankee that you should be prejudiced against him. He is a Southern man, a native of Virginia; an early settler in Arkansas, and an old citizen among us. The best of his life has been spent in trying to make us a better and happier people. He was here, a pioneer in the wilds of the West, enduring the hardships and privations of border-life long before these brainless, hissing goslings were hatched."

This appeal had the desired effect. The ruffians were shamed into silence, at least for a time.

"Fellow-citizens, Christian brethren, neighbors and friends," began the good man, seeming to forget that he had just been calumniated, mocked, and derided, "who, among you, looks upon me as an enemy? Where is the man, woman, or child, that I have wronged? During a long series of years have I not proved myself the friend of this community? If I have reproved, rebuked, admonished, and exhorted you, it has been because I loved you, wished you well, and sought to lead you into the way of life and salvation. Besides, am I not the friend of this country? Am I not the friend and lover of the South, and especially of the great Southwest? Am I not the firm friend, the long-tried friend, of Arkansas? If any of you dare say otherwise, I challenge you to speak. My countrymen, whatever my faults and imperfections may be, you know that I am true to this country and true to you. Then it is because I am your friend, and the friend of our common country, that I am also the friend and defender of the *Union*, — our ever-glorious and heaven-blessed UNION!"

The closing of the sentence, which should have elicited hearty applause, brought only another storm of hisses and howlings.

But, quailing not, nor in the least losing his perfect self-possession, the patriotic servant of God and of his country went on: "Believe me, fellow-citizens and friends, no greater calamity could befall the South — certainly none greater could happen to Arkansas — than a dissolution of the Union."

Now again, the brainless, brutal mob raged, raved, and rent the air with hideous yells, vulgar epithets, and cursing.

"You excite my sympathies rather than my indignation," calmly remarked the speaker, soon as the tumult had sufficiently subsided. "Ignorance," he added, "is more to be pitied than blamed."

"He insults your intelligence, gentlemen," cried out a secesh clergyman, who had followed his congregation from their own place of worship to see the Union preacher mobbed.

With this encouragement from a pulpit man, the ruffians began anew to threaten vengeance, and to call for tar and feathers.

"I wouldn't blame you," said the disloyal parson, again lifting up his hypocritical voice, "if you were to treat the old sinner to a cravat, made of hemp. Such a neck-tie, I imagine, would well become a Union preacher's complexion."

"Yes, let us hang him!" said a blackleg, in the midst of the disorderly throng, and who seemed to be the chief centre of attraction for the riotous, indecent, and turbulent part of the excited concourse.

"Hang him! hang him!" shouted a score of voices, taking their cue from the blackleg.

Still calm as a summer evening, the gray-haired patriot, casting a look of sorrow upon the disorderly rabble, said, —

"Misguided men, however unseemly this conduct may be, I pity you. Yes, down deep in my heart I pity you. Nor is there one among you whom I pity *more* than this poor traitor, who professes to be a gospel minister."

While uttering the last sentence, he pointed
his finger directly at the shameless clergyman,
who had just sought to instigate the mob to acts
of violence.   This sharp rebuke so incensed and
kindled the ire of the reverend traitor that he
went into a diabolical rage most shocking to
behold.   It seemed he would certainly explode!
— indeed, did explode in a tornado of wrathful
words, vulgar slang, and opprobrious epithets.

As soon as order was partially restored again,
the speaker said, —

"Why are the services of the sanctuary interrupted to-day?   Why have I not been allowed
to proceed as usual in my ministrations?   Why
am I threatened with mob-violence ?   And why
have I been told this morning, by a committee
of professedly Christian men, that I must change
my sentiments, renounce my opinions, or cease
to occupy the pulpit?   Yes, I am to be turned
out of the pulpit, in which I have so long labored to promote the cause of Christ, the cause
of truth and virtue, to build up society, and
elevate humanity.   What is my offence ?"

"Preaching politics !" cried out a political

demagogue, standing up before the minister with a beet-red nose, and so drunk he could scarcely see.

"Ministers of the gospel," chimed in the rebel clergyman, who had just been boiling over with fury, "have no business taking anything into the pulpit but religion."

"The heaven-appointed watchman on Zion's walls, if true to his trust," replied the speaker, "is ever vigilant to guard and defend, not only the interests of religion and of the Church, but also the interests of his government and country. For, while he is a minister of Christ, he is likewise a patriot. While he is a herald of the cross, he is at the same time a citizen, sharing the benefits, and enjoying the protection, of civil government.

"Put him down! put him down!" shouted a stentorian voice.

"Drag him out! drag him out!" bawled another.

"Damn the Yankee Government!" cried a third.

"Hurrah for the Southern Confederacy!" shouted the red-nosed political demagogue.

"Hurrah! hurrah! hurrah!" went up like a tempest from the loud-mouthed rabble.

Paying no attention to this interruption, further than to wait for a chance to be heard, the speaker went on : —

"It is, I grant," said he, mildly, "the chief duty of the minister to preach the gospel of the Son of God, and call sinners to repentance; but has he, therefore, nothing to do with temporal affairs? Why should he be thought less interested than other men in the salvation of the republic, and in the prosperity of the commonwealth ?"

"We must keep politics out of the pulpit!" spake another tory clergyman.

"Nothing is foreign to the pulpit," responded the occupant of the desk, "which belongs to humanity. Nor should any topic be excluded therefrom that is calculated to honor God, elevate and enlighten mankind."

"All that's but sophistry! sheer sophistry !" exclaimed the tory parson, anxious to annoy and interrupt the speaker.

"The minister of Jesus," continued Rev. Elmore, "lives and labors to make the world better, wiser, and happier. He seizes with avidity every opportunity for doing good, whether spiritual or temporal. He is ready to lay hold of any plan, to exhaust every scheme, to seek out and perfect any contrivance, whereby the interests of humanity, the interests of religion, the interests of truth and virtue, may be subserved."

"We've heard enough!" exclaimed the bleareyed, red-nosed politician, impatiently; "we've heard enough!" he repeated, adding a profane oath, which we prefer to omit.

"It is the duty of the incumbent of the pulpit," said the speaker, heeding not the vaporing of the demagogue toper, "to make himself felt in all the relations of life; throughout all the ramifications of society, and in every laudable enterprise looking to the amelioration of our race."

"He has enough to do to preach the gospel," observed one of the secesh clergymen, with affected gravity, and a look of hypocritical piety.

"While he contends earnestly for the faith once delivered to the saints," responded the speaker, "he should plead with no less zeal for the principles of liberty, justice, and humanity."

"There, — listen at that!" cried out a fire-eater; "*liberty*, he says. Aha! he means that the niggers are to be free! He's nothing but an abolitionist."

"Hang him! shoot him! tar and feather him!" cried the mob. And now another rush was made toward the pulpit, by the infuriated ruffians; whereupon, Malvin again drew his revolver.

One of the secesh preachers, who stood near him, the same who recommended hemp for the Union minister, seized the weapon in Malvin's hand, and attempted to wrench it from his grasp; in so doing he caused the pistol to go off. The ball passed through the Rev. traitor's hand, and, thence glancing along the side of his head, took one of his ears nearly off, and, passing on in an upward direction, lodged in the body of the blackleg, who had just mounted on a pew behind the secesh preacher, taking him, as a sailor would say, between wind and water.

This tragical affair produced an indescribable scene of confusion. Women shrieked, men were terrified, and a general stampede straightway ensued. Nor could anything have been more ludicrous to look upon. Many rushed for the doors, while others, in their great haste to escape, went heels over head out at the windows.

The church was soon cleared; and the people, having got a thorough panic, ran in every direction, like a frightened herd of wild cattle. The blackleg, who carried off the lead, went out crying "*Murder*," as loud as he could bellow. And the unlucky clergyman, making sure he had received a mortal wound, made all possible speed toward home, calling on God at every jump to have mercy on his poor soul.

Malvin took his aged pastor by the arm and proposed to accompany him home.

"Have you another pistol, my boy?" inquired the hoary-headed patriot; "we may be attacked on our way."

" A capital one ; " answered Malvin, taking from his bosom a splendid revolver, which the minister took, saying, —

" There is a time for praying, there is a time for preaching, and there has now come a time for shooting."

CHAPTER IV.

"How wisdom and folly meet, mix, and unite;
How virtue and vice blend their black and white!"

GOD never intended men to be equal. There must be an aristocracy," said Macqueen, addressing his wife, and putting on an air and tone of ostentation.

"Aristocracy!" answered she, scornfully; "I can respect aristocracy of intellect; and I admire aristocracy in virtue, in amiability, in nobility of nature; but an aristocracy built on dollars and dimes, or on slaves, houses, and lands, which any dunce, born to good luck, may possess, I hate, loathe, and abhor!"

"I'm in no mood for argument. You delight to dash my highest hopes and brightest dreams

to the ground. I cherish but a laudable ambition, and, but for you, would mount up to distinction."

"Wondrous pity that I should pull you back!
I count not that a laudable ambition, my husband, which aims at sheer selfish ends. To
achieve personal aggrandizement, you would
not hesitate to bring wretchedness and misery
upon millions of our race. For your own glory,
you would spill seas of blood! Such an ambition is unworthy a true man, unworthy of a
noble mind; it is even Satanic, and merits only
scorn and contempt."

"Of what avail is all this raillery?"

"Call it raillery if you like. A just indignation deserves a better name."

"When I see its justice, I will then christen
it something else."

"The blackness of the treason that would destroy a government like this, and sunder our
glorious Union, no tongue can tell, no pencil
can paint. The arch apostate, that rebelled in
heaven, conspiring against the Almighty, and
who, in reckless malice, would fain have de-

throned the Most High, scarce exceeded in wickedness this nefarious treason!"

"And still you rail!"

"Suppose you succeed in laying in ruins the fair fabric of this mighty Republic, how much better off will you be than Milton's fallen angels when they had reached the depths of perdition? But, like them, perhaps, you'd 'rather reign in hell than serve in heaven.'"

"Come, say no more."

"To call such men disloyal is not enough; they are a brotherhood of fiends! And may perdition enlarge itself to give them room!"

"How strangely to my ears sound such words from you, Florence!"

"Why should I not feel indignant and aggrieved? Who are your accomplices in this Satanic work? Herds of vicious, idle, dissipated men, and profligate wretches, who have nothing to lose by change and revolution. These, led on by disappointed politicians and unprincipled demagogues, are your chief abettors in sowing the seeds of sedition, kindling the fires of civil war, and rolling on the dark and desolating wave of revolution."

"Why will you thus go on hurling bitter words? You have ceased to be yourself, Florence."

"Little wonder!"

"I pray you put by that frown, and speak to me in gentler tones. Remember that 'words fitly spoken are like apples of gold in pictures of silver.'"

"My husband, had I loved you less, your fault in this could not have grieved me so. The light of your eye has ever been the sunshine of my heart. But I cannot be blind to your terrible sin. Oh, let me persuade you, by all that's sacred, by all we each hold dear, to abandon this wicked, reckless project of revolution. Oh, I entreat you, be not partaker in the guilt of those who are insanely kindling a fire which all the waters of the deep seas cannot quench!—a fire which will surely devour this fair land, and make it a desert waste!"

"She may predict the truth," said the husband to himself, turning away dejected; "but to retract is now impossible," he added, mentally. Directly turning again to his wife, and putting on a look of utter wretchedness, he said, " To own the truth, Florence, so far have I committed myself in this affair, I cannot now recede from the unfortunate position I occupy. Revolution is determined on ; I am sworn, and cannot recant."

" Merciful Heaven ! "   exclaimed the wife, clasping her hands convulsively, and in the agony of grief.

" To do otherwise, at this juncture, than go forward," said he, " would cost me my life."

" Oh, tell me not so, my husband!   Oh, it cannot be that you are involved in a scheme of treason so dreadful, so deep and dark, that you cannot extricate yourself!"

" Peace, Florence ! I pray you, peace !"

"At all hazards abandon the conspiracy at once and forever ! "

" The nature and extent of this revolutionary plot you little comprehend, Florence. Nor have you dreamed of the reckless determination with which it is to be carried out. Rather than fail, the most desperate measures are to be resorted to."

"Alas, and I have not known the worst!"

"Let us hope for the best," said the husband, evidently much moved, yet striving to appear composed.

"Hope? there is no hope!" exclaimed the weeping wife; "all is darkness and despair."

Macqueen, in character, was a real Southern-er, — a Southerner of the higher class. He was a man of hot blood, quick temper, and ungoverned passions. He was kind and cruel; polite and rude; magnanimous and supercilious; chivalric and pusillanimous.

A being of impulse, he seldom paused to reflect, and rarely looked before he leaped. By nature rash and precipitant, had he possessed a lower grade of intellect, his life would have been one of broils and combat. And, notwithstanding his fair mental capacity, and his respectable literary attainments, his animal passions were dominant, and, for the most part, controlled his actions.

With a hearty good-will he would either bless or curse you as the humor might take him. He cherished a keen sense of honor; but had a very blunt perception as to what true honor consisted in. He respected religion, but profaned the name of God. Feared hell, but loved to serve the devil. He worshipped a fine horse; liked dogs; was deferential to ministers; polite to ladies; and always had an eye for the cream-colored creole in crinoline.

Mrs. Macqueen was a native of Alabama, and altogether Southern in her manners and education, but had become something *more* than the real Southern lady. She was a woman of thought and reflection. Yet, at the same time, was not without the fire peculiar to Southern blood. She was quick, ardent, sensitive, and sometimes fearfully impetuous. When unexcited, few women or few men exercised more philosophy. And with a strong intellect she united a warm and generous heart.

To her husband's whims and wayward inclinations she had been habitually indulgent, — even to a fault. But touching the question of the Union, she was inflexible from the beginning, and utterly abhorred the madness of secession. This brought their proud spirits and fiery natures into frequent and sometimes·terrible collision.

CHAPTER V.

"When vice prevails, and impious men bear sway,
The post of honor is a private station."

SANGUINARY revolutions seldom fail to bring to the surface the vilest, most reckless, and abandoned class of men. This was particularly exemplified at Platte City, in the infamous career of a despicable wretch, whose name was Ironsides, but more commonly called Ironheart, on account of his great cruelty to his slaves. He was a man of colossal stature, stooping figure, and by no means comely features. Skin, swarthy; hair, coarse and grizzled; eyes, black as night, and almost hidden beneath a heavy, shaggy brow, such as pirates are wont to wear.

No man could have been more universally despised than was Ironsides. Black and white,

6*

male and female, rich and poor, held him in great detestation and utter abhorrence. By those who knew him best, he was said to be without a redeeming trait.

That humanity is capable of such depravity, we may feel some reluctance to admit; for it certainly would be comforting to think that there is something good in every man. But if there was any mixture of the angel in the soul of this human brute, no one, it seems, had ever found it out.

Yet, reprobate as he was, depraved and vile as everybody admitted him to be, in the commotions of the country he was directly brought to the surface, — and even lifted above it, — exalted to an eminence, where he soon gained sufficient influence, by the help of the Devil, to wield despotic power for a time, and rule the people with a rod of iron.

"*For desperate times we need desperate men,*" said the plotting rebels who pulled the wires behind the curtain. "Let us give Ironsides the reins, at least while the storm lasts. Rest assured he'll quickly rid the country of Union men and abolitionists."

A Vigilant Committee had already been appointed; but as they had only hung and shot some half-dozen Union men within a fortnight, they were reckoned, by the impatient chivalry, as quite too lenient. Secession was moving too tardily. To remedy this matter, it was now deemed expedient to make Ironsides the " *Head Chief*," of the vigilant committee.

Soon after his appointment to this post of honor, over the Border-ruffian Sanhedrim, the names of several prominent citizens were written down for ostracism, and among them was the name of a descendant of the New York Knickerbockers,—an eccentric bachelor, slightly turned upon the shady side of life. He was a man of lofty bearing and decidedly aristocratic mould, a fine scholar, possessed rare scientific attainments, and was by profession a lawyer. Highly-organized, and made out of Nature's finest material, he was consequently sensitive and excitable. Thus constituted, he was quick to resent gross insults and injuries, although habitually kind and conciliatory.

His utter scorn of the brutal mob, the vulgar

herd, and unwashed rabble, he seldom cared to disguise. You should have seen him, one day, as he stood upon the curbstone, a few paces from the threshold of his office, gazing with kindling ire upon an armed band of marauding rebels who were ostentatiously parading up and down the streets. As appears the sky when it gathers blackness and tempest, so looked Knickerbocker's face, darkened with wrath. And as the lightning leaps from the fretted bosom of the thunder-cloud, so flashed the fires of indignation from his blazing eye. Manifestly the spirit of the hurricane and of the whirlwind was there, and with difficulty held in restraint; but the storm was not yet allowed to burst forth. At length, turning about, he walked into his office, resolving in his mind to keep a bridle upon his tongue, if not a padlock on his mouth.

Upon his table had just been laid an unsealed letter by an unobserved messenger.

"A missive, eh!" said he to himself; "from what quarter, I wonder?"

Taking up, and opening the note, he began to read audibly:—

"'Mr. Knickerbocker,—Sir: as chairman of the Vigilant Committee of Platte City,'"—Here, suddenly pausing, he indignantly exclaimed, "Viligant Committee! An infernal banditti, who take it upon themselves to say who shall be hanged; who banished the country; who tarred and feathered; or who jay-hawked! Heavens! I'm highly honored! What have such cut-throats to do with me?"

While thus exploding, he dashed some two or three times across the floor, from one side of his office to the other, seemingly unconscious of where he was or what he did. After a while, calming himself a little, he again read, "'It is made my duty to acquaint you with the sentiments of the Committee, touching your position, and what is required of you.'" Again abruptly breaking off and kindling into a passion, he wheeled round and began striding the floor, reiterating, in the most excited manner, the last read sentence,—"'Touching your position, and what is required of you!'

"The impudent hounds! The unhung assassins and thieves! The hell-deserving fiends!

Oh, there's no use hunting epithets, — I can't do the demons justice!"

Again he paused to read : —

" 'Permit me, sir, to say, that your queer, uneuphonious name has led to the suspicion ' — Queer, uneuphonious name?" he iterated, with astonishment and disgust; "what miserable taste the fellow has! — Knick — er — bock — er, — was there ever a better sounding name than that?"

Again reading: " 'Has led to the suspicion that your political faith may not be entirely orthodox.'

" Prodigious! Have I lived to see the day when a man's name may place him under ban?" Then again reading: " 'We are every day the more convinced that the foreign population in our midst constitute a dangerous element of society.'

" Oh, ho! they've set me down for a foreigner, because, forsooth, my name's Knickerbocker! — The blockheads!"

Still perusing the letter: " 'And it is now deemed expedient to test their loyalty to the

South, by requiring them to take up arms against the North.'

"O magnanimous Committee! This is something worthy of Southern chivalry," he exclaimed with bitter irony; then went on with the letter: "'Now, sir, to come at once to an ultimatum, you must straightway join the army of the South; or forthwith make tracks for the North.'

"The Devil!" he exclaimed, unable to restrain his wrath any longer; and, tearing the offensive letter to pieces, flung the fragments to the winds, saying,—

"Let the dog-star rage! Let the caldron boil, froth, and foam! Stir in foul treason, treachery, lechery, and all vileness and all villany! Satan admire me, if the infernal clan haven't kindled a fire that will smoke their own eyes! Heaven grant them good speed hellwards! By Saint Paul, perdition shall hold them all! For sure as old Hangie wears horns, they are the Devil's own!"

At this juncture, an intimate acquaintance, Mr. Clifton Clifford, entered the office, and, seeing his friend in a fume, said,—

"Pray, what has happened, Mr. Knicker-bocker?"

"Oh, these provoking rebels, instigated by a legion of devils, have just struck a lucifer match against the saltpetre of my combustible na-ture! So, of course, I went off, throwing shot and shell into the air frightfully; and the only pity is, that I've killed nobody."

"But what, in the name of wonder, has tran-spired to set you in such a flutter?"

"Why, sir, I've just been honored with a note from the Great Moguls of this part of Rebel-dom, — devildom, — coolly informing me that I've got to leave the country, or join the secesh army!"

"And is that all?"

"All? Count you that a small affair? Who ever heard before of such an outrage?"

"Be comforted, my dear fellow; I've just received a missive of the same kind."

"There's a vast deal of comfort in that! And what do you propose to do about it?"

"Oh, we must bend a little to the wind; wear a nose of wax for convenience, — incline it

toward the South; put on a make-believe face,
— and talk secesh."

"Would I be forced to seem the thing I
scorn?"

"Oh, that's but strategy. When the Moguls
take snuff, you and I must sneeze."

"I'll be shot first!"

"Have your choice, Mr. Knickerbocker. A
man of my complexion never dies a martyr."

"Our murdered patriots shall be avenged!—
Blood for blood! I've sworn it!"

"My dear sir, forget not where you are."

"Let traitors do their worst; I'll fight them
while I've life and breath!"

"Keep cool,—I entreat you, keep cool."

"Talk to a volcano about keeping cool,—the
red-mouthed volcano!"

"The fellow's going mad!" said Clifford,
aside; "I fear he'll get himself into trouble."

"Would to God I were another Vesuvius!"
continued the excited patriot, "and that the
whole generation of vile traitors were packed
and cribbed in Charleston. I'd belch a torrent
of consuming, hissing, liquid fire on that Sodom,

till it was buried a thousand fathoms deeper than Pompeii or Herculaneum!"

"Hold, sir, I pray you, hold!"

"The last traitor should perish,—miserably perish! Blistering cinders, lurid flames, and rolling, quivering waves of dire combustion should overwhelm and fry every treacherous rascal of them to a crackling!"

"Misery and death!" whispered Clifford to himself; "he'll surely be shot before he's done raving."

"Not one of all the God-forgotten and heaven-abhorred reprobates should escape! 'Neath melted rocks, and the crisped, spewed-up earth and ore, I'd entomb them beyond the hope of a resurrection."

"My dear sir, you rage like the sea."

"Let me be the raging sea, or another Noah's flood, that I may drown the whole rebel brood!" And, wheeling about, he dashed out upon the street like a madman.

"Wild as the wind!" exclaimed his friend. "I, too, love my country; but am not over-anxious to prove it by putting my head into a lion's mouth, or pulling the Devil by the tail."

CHAPTER VI.

"O God, what mischiefs work the wicked ones;
Heaping confusion on their own heads thereby!"

————

IN a sequestered part of Platte City, or rather in the suburbs of the town, there was a verdant spot, where nestled a pretty little vine-clad cottage, embowered 'neath umbrageous forest trees, luxuriantly clothed with deep-green glossy leaves. Around the window casements, and about the eaves, I have seen creeping the ivy-green and honeysuckle. What a tempting, ruby cup of nectar the latter offered to the humming-bird! a feathered beauty of exquisite plumage, dyed in the hues of the rainbow. How oft with delight I've gazed upon it, while poised in air upon its delicate wings, and sipping delicious wine from the blushing blossom goblet, which seemed formed and fashioned for it alone.

About the door, on either side, and overhead, you might have seen the morning-glory unfold its beauty, — pink and purple, sky-blue and purest white, giving an air of taste, sweetness, and comfort to the humble dwelling. This was the domicile of Parson Southdown, the only loyal minister then in the community, or in all the region round.

The day of which I am about to speak was one of tumult and excitement in Platte City. Companies of armed men, gangs of ruffians, gentlemen and scallawags, women and children, old men and boys, white trash and black trash, were pouring into town from every quarter.

Mrs. Southdown was sitting alone at her front window, and looking out with a sad heart and melancholy expression upon the swelling throng, thinking of her far-off New-England home, and rueing the day on which she had consented to go to the land of the oppressed.

"Alas!" said she, "what's to become of us in this lawless country, where the mob rules and vilest men bear sway?"

Just at this moment, Knickerbocker entered the gate-way.

"Good-morning, Uncle!" said Mrs. South-down, speaking from the open window, "I've been wishing you'd come; I'm so lonesome to-day."

"You may soon wish me gone again," responded he, and coming in with a twinkle of humor in his eye; "for I've got old Nick in me to-day, big as a lion and savage as a regiment of tigers."

"Oh, I hope not. Pray, who has crossed you?"

"Who? Just look at these Border-ruffians, pouring down like driftwood and floating trash on a swollen stream, just after a deluging rain. One might think purgatory had taken a vomit. Such a generation of vipers is enough to cross St. Peter."

"What we cannot cure we must endure, Uncle."

"I have endured everything, and held my tongue and temper marvellously. But now to see those ragamuffins coming in to disturb the

7*

peace of society provokes me.   Well, well, 'tis said, 'Every dog must have his day;' and I suppose every day must have its dog.   This one has a good many, and all sorts.   Where is Parson Southdown?"

"Gone to the post-office, I think."

"The mail of late lags behind.   An overload of bad report, mixed up with rebel lies, perhaps, makes it stick in the mud."

"If rebel lies had weight, Uncle, Missouri mail-coaches, these unblessed days, would sure break down."

"Ha! the very earth would reel, crack, and cave in."

"I dread to hear the news that's next to salute our ears."

"To borrow trouble is but to tickle the devil. Come good, come ill, fortune's wheel turn which way it will, keep you a cheerful heart, Amelia."

"Did you hear the uproar on the street last night, Uncle?"

"Hear it? My ears are not made of lead, nor quite deaf to what might wake the dead. Such an everlasting din was kept up the live-long night, I thought surely hell was empty, and that all the yelling demons were here in Platte City."

"What could it mean, — have you any conjecture ?"

"Why, it meant that His Majesty, Auld Nickaben, had some special business on hand, and must needs marshal his Border-ruffian clans."

"They whooped and howled most hideously."

"Just like any other gang of prowling beasts, hungry wolves, or hooting owls. That horrid yell, which split the ear of midnight, was in honor, I imagine, of the Swamp Angels, who came into town at a late hour in the evening, for the purpose of being organized into a guerrilla band."

"Swamp Angels? Pray, what are they ?"

"Animals with two legs and no feathers."

"Not flying angels, then, it would seem ? "

"Unfledged as yet; though in the wind you'd think them winged, their tattered garments, many-colored rags, and dishevelled hair such a strange fluttering make. A herd of miserable creatures they are that inhabit a pestiferous region in a bend of the river among dismal swamps.

> 'Their only wish and their only prayer,
> Their only hope, and their only care,
> For the present world, or the world to come,
> Is a string of fish and a jug of rum.'

"Admirable material for guerrillas! Of such stuff, I suppose, they should be made."

" Your husband is returning."

" Has the paper, I perceive."

" If I read his face aright, there's something more in the wind than the perfume of sweet flowers. There's a cloud upon his brow and displeasure in his eye."

" Good-morning, Mr. Knickerbocker!" said Southdown, as he approached the threshold, making an effort to maintain his usual air, and accustomed cheerful greeting.

" We've already read the news, parson," facetiously remarked Knickerbocker, "in your speaking eye and tell-tale face, ere your lips could part, or your tongue wag to tell us what it is."

" Say, then, if you can divine, what news do I bring ?"

"Nothing, I ween, to provoke our laughter. I'll guess the devil has broke his halter."

"Right for once, Mr. Knickerbocker."

"Pray, let us hear," said Mrs. Southdown, impatiently.

"Fort Sumter has fallen!"

"Alas! and what will happen next?" exclaimed the lady, raising her hands in consternation, as if expecting, the next moment, to feel the nation's convulsions, as well she might after such an event.

Knickerbocker assumed a similar attitude, and stood for some moments profoundly silent, and without the sign of motion or the movement of a muscle.

"A sad affair!" observed the parson. "The infatuated beings know not what they do."

"Perdition take the whole traitor crew!" said Knickerbocker, with emphasis; and, becoming much excited, began to promenade to and fro across the floor with nervous and rapid strides.

"Patience, Uncle, patience!" insisted Mrs. Southdown. "It is a time for humility and prayer."

"If there ever was a time to curse and swear," whispered Knickerbocker to himself, "it strikes me that it's about now." Then turning to Mrs. Southdown, he said, "Well, well; I'll take it patiently, since you advise me so, Amelia."

"We may now look for the transpiring of startling events," remarked Southdown. "By this time," continued he, "the Northern heart's on fire! Yankee blood boils in Yankee veins!"

"So it does," said Knickerbocker aside; "mine boils me out of my boots,—almost!"

"At the same time," continued the parson, "all Dixie's in a flame,—a consuming, wide-wasting flame! Southern blood goes galloping through Southern veins, scalding hot!"

"From blind passion and bad whiskey," responded Knickerbocker dryly.

"Here comes my colored friend," said Parson Southdown, looking toward the door. "Walk in, Uncle Ned."

"Black outside, but not so dark within as many a man of fairer skin," soliloquized Knickerbocker, mentally, as the slave entered, hat in hand, and bowing at every step with all the politeness, if not with all the grace of a French dancing-master.

-" Massa Soufdown," began the colored man, " I's actily furd you's gwien to ave tribulation-some times. For I tells ye what, de Ole Boy's onhobbled! You jist orter see de white trash dat's crowdin' 'bout de taverns, and fillin' de rum-holes, an swearin' like de bery heathens!"

"A bad set of fellows, I dare say, Uncle Ned," replied the parson.

" De wustest men dis side of de bad place!" continued the slave; "an' de streets am chock-full ob dem. All de unhung, an' all what de Debil hain't kotch, hab come to town! I pray de Lor A'mighty dat de yarth may open an' swaller dem up as Jonah did de whale!"

" What are they going to do, Uncle Ned?"

" Why, Massa, der's nuffin bad an' bomnable dat da won't do. An' dat ole sarvant ob de Debil, what da call Ironheart, he say dat Parson Soufdown ab no business comin' down Souf no 'ow. An' furdermore, he sweared by all dat's good, an' all dat's bad, and all dat's wus an' more wusser, dat da'll hang Parson Soufdown, an' all de dam Yankees whomsumebber, dat dar stan up for de star an' stripes."

"The miserable traitor !"

"An' jis den, dat ole Judas, preacher Snooks, who am de Debil's own mouf-piece, steps right up an' said, says he, 'We'll hang dat Union preacher higher nor Haman!' How high da hung dat gent'man dis darky can't 'zactly say, sar. But I kinder 'spect it wor purty well up in de ar."

"Ah, Uncle Ned, bad men will get their deserts, by and by," remarked the parson; "but don't be alarmed about me. Depend upon it, I wasn't born to be hung."

"Oh, ho! Massa, but dat doesn't signify nuffin; dem ar grillers nebber stops for dat. Da nebber 'quires who am born for de gallus, or who for de tar an' fedders. De bestest peoples am what da sarve de wustest."

"Uncle Ned understands the reprobates," observed Southdown to Knickerbocker. "He gives them their true character."

"May de good Lor A'mighty 'ave mercy on us pour critters!" added the slave; "for de great red Dragon 'ave shuck off him chain, an's gwien 'bout killin' an' debowerin! It make de berry hair ob my head stan' straight on eand!"

"What! your kinky wool stand on end, Uncle Ned?" questioned the parson, humorously.

"Oh, but you doesn't comprehension me. I speaks diabolical."

"Diabolical! Mercy on us!" exclaimed Knickerbocker mischievously.

"Uncle Ned means parabolical," explained the parson.

"Parzactly! dat am de word. I couldn't jist git him by de right name. Well, den, I's 'bout done dischargin' my duty. And now I prays de good Lor A'mighty dat we all mout be saved, 'spacially from de jay-hawkers and de swamp angels, an' from de everlastin' clutches ob de Ole Boy, who am gwien 'bout seekin to debower! An' furdermore, may de good bein' 'bove de sky bless an' marcifully presarve you an' me an' all de dam Yankees ebrywhur on de face ob de wide yearth, world widout eand."

Saying which, the good-hearted slave bowed adieu, and turned about to depart.

"We are greatly obliged to you, Uncle Ned," said the parson; "call whenever you can."

"You's de fust white man dat eber say dat much to dis poor darky, — 'Bleige to ye, Uncle Ned.' Oh, dat am music to my yur, sweeter dan de sound of de bugle horn!"

Again bowing adieu, he advanced toward the door, when another thought struck him. Turning round, he said, "Now you isn't gwien to tell Massa or Misses bout what I's been tellin ye, is ye?"

"By no means, Uncle Ned," replied Parson Southdown; "rest easy on that score."

"But I's kinder jubersom ob dis ar gentman."

"What, of me?" said Knickerbocker; "how is that?"

"I tells you case why. I 'members one day as dis darky you wor passin by, ye kinder snuff de win', an say 'De odor ob de gentman ob color ar mighty undegreable.'"

"Ah, Uncle Ned, I'm quite over that now. In my nostrils the poor slave smells so much better than his traitor master that I begin to relish the odor amazingly."

"When dis darky you de better knows, he'll all de better smell in your nose."

Now, making his last bow, Uncle Ned withdrew, doubtless blessed with a sense of duty done.

The concourse upon the streets, already immense, was every moment increasing. Though a busy season of the year, yet almost all business was laid aside and neglected. The blood of the Border-ruffian chivalry was up ; war was in their hearts, and whiskey running down their throats. News of the fall of Sumter had rapidly spread, and was now on every tongue. As cups and canteens went round, enthusiasm kindled ; blood waxed warmer, and tongues grew longer.

"Only see," said Mrs. Southdown, "how the armed ruffians are still coming into town ; what do they mean ?"

"They are brought together to-day by various motives," replied her husband ; "one is, to rejoice over the fall of Sumter. Another is, to organize more jay-hawking and guerrilla companies. Still another object, and, perhaps, the leading one, is to get up a new furor in favor of secession, and to deter loyal citizens from expressing their sentiments, and opposing their project of taking Missouri out of the Union."

"While these desperate men," said Mrs. Southdown, "are every day robbing and murdering loyal citizens, wherever they find them, what security have we?"

"I must admit, we are not safe. But how shall we help ourselves? I see no remedy unless we leave the country, and there is hazard in that. Every family that have yet attempted to leave the State, and carry with them their personal property, have been robbed, either by their disloyal neighbors, or by the roving bands of jay-hawkers that are infesting every part of the country."

"I've just bethought me what we'd better do," said the eccentric Knickerbocker; "all things, you know, are honorable in war."

"Not *all* things, Uncle;" objected Mrs. Southdown.

"I mean honorable, as the world goes. This,

then, I propose: that we, for a time, dissemble, turn secesh, and pretend to be on the side of the traitors. Thus we may not only make ourselves safe in person and property, but, meanwhile, play spy upon the disloyal rascals. And when the government sends troops into the State to protect loyal citizens and crush the rebellion, which no doubt will be done after a while, then we can show our colors, and come out upon the black-hearted traitors."

" Oh, but that would be deception!" exclaimed Mrs. Southdown, chidingly.

" Knaves are only fit to be deceived," rejoined Knickerbocker.

" Say not so, Uncle."

" To be honest with these rogues, conspirators, and assassins is but to cast pearls before swine."

" Let us be honest, Uncle, if the stars fall."

" First, let us be honest to ourselves, Amelia, while we're among wolves."

" How differently you talk, Uncle, from what you ever did before. Why, it was but yesterday you were ready to die for your principles."

" So I was; but to-day I'm not quite so much

8*

in the spirit of dying as I am of killing some-
body. ·I must live to be the death of some of
these assassins who have murdered their loyal
neighbors."

"Heaven help us! I know not what we'd
better do."

"There are dark plots at work, perfidious designs and infernal machinations going on; we
must find them out, and, if possible, expose and
defeat them."

"If such a course were justifiable," observed
the parson, "it would certainly be hazardous,
surrounded as we are by treacherous and reckless men, who scruple not at anything."

"I will press neither of you into the scheme;
but I'm bound to try my hand, for the first time
in my life, at a game of duplicity."

"Surely, Uncle, you cannot be serious."

"Rest assured I am. Say no more. I'll go
mingle with the mob; pat the dogs on the back,
and be the fiercest hound in the pack!"

CHAPTER VII.

E recur again to the persecutions of the youthful patriot, Adrian Malvin, and his venerable pastor, Rev. Elmore. And here we resume a leading-thread of our narrative, which, the reader may remember, we dropped at the conclusion of the third chapter.

The mob, not satisfied with their disgraceful conduct at the house of God on Sabbath morning, renewed the riot in the evening, about sunset, by surrounding the parsonage, and hurling stones, brickbats, and other missiles against the windows and doors, and, meanwhile, pouring forth torrents of curses and profane oaths, swearing vengeance against all Union men and opposers of secession.

Anticipating an assault upon his dwelling, the parson had taken the precaution to send his family away during the afternoon; but determined, himself, to resist as long as he could any attempt on the part of the mob to enter his house. Malvin pledged himself to stand by and render him all the assistance within his power.

On seeing the rioters coming, they had hastened to barricade the doors and windows as best they could, then, seizing their weapons, had taken their positions, bravely resolved, if the ruffians broke in, to make it cost them dearly.

The assault was terrific; and in a few minutes the windows were demolished, and the front-door wellnigh battered down. After showering missiles of every description upon the house till they were tired, the mob desisted for a time, and went off to a drinking-saloon. Taking advantage of the suspension of hostilities, Malvin and the parson went vigorously to work to strengthen their barricade, by piling up furniture against the doors and windows.

Three-quarters of an hour had scarcely elapsed when the vile clan returned, and more turbulent, profane, and boisterous than before. This time, the mob was led by a notorious guerrilla chief, who, with his murderous band, had just arrived from a marauding expedition, and the same who, but a few days before, had pursued Malvin into the mountains with the design of taking his life.

The attack was now made with much greater violence than at first, and the door and barricade directly gave way.

The guerrilla chief, ambitious to display his bravery, and eager to wreak vengeance upon Malvin, whom he hated, no less for his amiability and refinement of manners than for his patriotism, rushed in, but scarcely had passed the threshold, when a ball from Malvin's revolver brought the reckless wretch sprawling upon the floor, bleeding like a slaughtered bullock.

Parson Elmore, following suit, put a bullet in the brain of the next man. Other ruffians, who were crowding in, now took the hint, and, quickly wheeling about, began to retreat; but some of them were a little too late to get out of harm's way; bang! bang! bang! went the six-shooters, and at each fire, a rascal came down, or else went off howling.

While this was transpiring, a gun was accidentally discharged in the midst of the throng outside, the contents of which lodged in the neck of one of the secesh clergymen who had come to see the fun. The Rev. traitor, taken on surprise, and hit in a tender spot, bellowed like a bull, and went off floundering through the crowd like a wounded buffalo in a bog.

At this juncture, amid such terrible disasters, a sudden panic seized the rabble, and a precipitant flight ensued.

"We are victorious, my brave boy!" said Parson Elmore; " and now is our time to decamp, while we are sure of our laurels as well as our lives."

"Decamp?—what, right at the moment of triumph?" questioned Malvin, in great astonishment.

"Know you not," replied the parson, " that these brutal wretches will directly rally again, and burn the house over our heads if we remain? and, perhaps, murder us in the most barbarous manner?"

"Ah, you are right, Parson," returned Malvin; "no doubt they will be more desperate than before."

"We ought not to throw away our lives," added the parson; "our country may need our services in the crisis through which it is now destined to pass."

They immediately set about making preparations for a flight into the hill-country adjacent to the village. Gathering up a roll of blankets, and filling a basket with provisions, they passed out through the back-yard under cover of the darkness, which had just set in, and made their escape unobserved.

It was doubtless fortunate for them that the mob delayed their attack till so near nightfall, for in open daylight they could by no possibility have made their escape, and would certainly have been brutally murdered.

After the persecuted men had got a little out of the village, a mile or more, they all at once perceived a bright light shining on the tree-tops before them; on looking round to see where it proceeded from, they beheld the parsonage wrapped in flames.

"Ah, just as I expected," remarked the parson, calmly; "the fiends have applied the torch! Well, let it burn; we've reason to be thankful for having escaped with our lives."

Knowing that it would be utterly unsafe to stop anywhere within the State, after what had happened, they concluded to make their way to Kansas, and so turned their course in a north-westerly direction, through an almost uninhabited region.

After travelling till about midnight, having reached the mountain wilds, they found themselves weary, and, calling a halt, spread their blankets, and laid themselves down to rest.

The mob, after burning the parsonage, and getting their destructive propensities fully excited, continued their work of malice and devastation to a frightful extent. They burnt the houses of all the Germans and free negroes for several miles round, and killed and crippled a number of the inmates. And, not content with even that, they hung two of the more moderate secessionists for opposing their madness. Such is the recklessness of brainless herds of men when once they begin the work of violence.

The refugees, who had fled to the hill-country in the direction of Kansas, rose up at dawn, refreshed and resolute, to resume their journey. Avoiding every human habitation, they kept in the dark forests and in the wilds of the mountains, still bearing to the northwest. About high noon they began to think about trying the contents of their basket. The better to relish their repast, they thought to seek out some spring or rivulet that would afford them the delicious beverage of clear, cold water. Turning down a deep ravine, in search of the sparkling fountain, they came suddenly upon a family of fugitive slaves, — a mulatto man and woman, with two little children. The fugitives were sitting upon the ground by a brooklet, dividing among themselves their last crust of bread.

At sight of the white men, the parents of the

9

children sprang wildly to their feet, and, taking an attitude of bold defiance, each brandished a gleaming blade of steel. Every look, attitude, and motion, evinced their readiness and determination to engage in a death-struggle.

"Pardon us!" cried the parson; "we are no slave-hunters."

"Thank God!" exclaimed the colored man; "ah! I now perceive you are not. Your gentle, kindly look and tone assure me that you have too much heart, too great a soul, to betray the poor slave who pants for liberty."

"And what have you to eat?" inquired the parson.

"This bit of crust you see here is between us and starvation;" answered the fugitive. "As for myself, I have not tasted food for three days; as you came up, I was about to put a few crumbs into my mouth, and let my wife and children eat the rest, and trust to Providence for the next meal."

"Well, you trusted not in vain," said the parson; "here comes Providence," pointing to the basket, as Malvin brought it forward, and began to spread out the delicious viands before the half-starved creatures.

"God is good, Simon," sobbed the woman, as she gazed upon this unexpected bounty; "I told you," added she, "Heaven wouldn't let our children starve." And tears of gratitude coursed their way down her dusky cheeks.

After all had satisfied their hunger, Simon entered into a recital of the circumstances connected with their escape.

"I," said he, "ran away from slavery more than a year ago, and have been ever since planning to get Hannah and the children away.

In Kansas, I rented a piece of land, and hired a horse and plough, and raised a crop, and then I built me a nice little cabin on the land; and soon as I'd got that done, I began to pray to the good Lord to guide me in getting my poor wife and children out of bondage. Pretty soon I started, trusting in God that I'd have success. I filled my knapsack with provisions enough to have supplied us all till we could have reached Kansas; but I had to hide it in the woods till I could find Hannah and the children; and I could only venture to look after them late at night. On my first attempt, I found out where she was, and got sight of her; but it was not until the next night that I secured a chance to speak with her. The whole thing was then soon arranged, and we on our way to Kansas; but when we reached the woods where I had buried my knapsack of provisions, I found that the wolves had dug it up, and devoured it all but that miserable crust we were about to eat when you came up. But we both felt confident that God would not let us perish."

"But your confidence wavered a little," remarked Malvin, "when you first got a glimpse of us."

"Yes," returned Simon, pensively; "I was sure the blood-hounds were upon us."

"What would you have done," inquired Malvin, "if, instead of us, it had been a gang of slave-hunters?"

"Hannah and I had made up our minds, at the very outset, that if we were pursued, we'd never be taken alive. Before leaving Kansas, I procured these weapons. which you saw in our hands. We were resolved, if attacked, circumstances be what they might, to fight to the very death. And we had further agreed, that if the odds should be greatly against us, and there should seem an utter impossibility for us to defend ourselves, that we would, right at the outset, take the lives of our dear children, — that they might be saved, at all events, from dragging out a miserable existence in a state of slavery."

"Do you think that would have been right, Simon ?" asked Parson Elmore.

"Yes," said the fugitive, firmly; "I think it would have been right, and but doing our duty to our children. I know what slavery is; death is to be preferred before it. It is only the very ignorant who can patiently endure the sufferings and degradation of slavery."

It might be here observed, that Simon and Hannah were altogether more intelligent than a majority of slaves, and far more intelligent than a large majority of "the white trash" of the Slave States. They used none of the low language nor barbarous pronunciation, peculiar to the lower grade of slaves and ignorant whites.

"Hannah had a very hard lot," continued Simon; "she has always been sickly; yet she was kept constantly at the hardest kind of work, and always hired out to wash and drudge, black boots and harness horses, winter and summer, and night and day, if occasion required; and that, to support two lazy, idle, dissipated young men. Hannah was the only slave the family ever owned. And for the last three years, all the family have been dead, but these two lounging, drunken loafers. What she earns has been for years their entire dependence for support. And they were already talking of selling her children, because of being hard pressed for spending-money. I only wish we could have got their two horses; they have a good horse apiece to spree round on, which is the only property they now own.

Just at this moment, a gruff, coarse voice called out from the top of the hill,—

"By jing! there they are now!"

Instantly looking up, Simon recognized the

two profligate young men, of whom he had just been speaking. They were mounted on their horses, and each was carrying a rifle.

Simon instinctively clutched his weapon, but the next instant looked at the parson, as if for counsel.

"There," exclaimed Hannah, in a suppressed voice, "are the wretches who call themselves my masters. Have we to fight our own battle, Simon? If so, let us be ready."

"Look you here," whispered the parson, showing the pistol in his bosom; "you keep perfectly still, and let this young man and myself manage it. Malvin, now let us put on as much of a swaggering air and tone as we can, and they will readily conclude that we have caught the fugitives; and thus may we get into close quarters with them, so that their guns will have no advantage over our pistols."

"The first nigger that runs," said Tom Bolton, the older one of the two slave-hunters, "I'll blow his brains out!"

"There's Hannah's husband," said the other with an oath; "we'll get at least a hundred dollars for taking him back."

"But there are two white men! who can they be?" said the older to the younger.

Malvin, now rising to his feet, said,—

"What are you going to give us for finding your niggers?"

"Oho! you caught them, eh?" responded Tom Bolton. "Well, we'll reward you, of course."

And at once dismounting and hitching their horses, they came forward, and, setting down their guns, took out a rope to tie the fugitives.

"Ah, ha, you jade!" said Tom, in a most tantalizing manner; "you got caught, did you? How many hundred lashes do you think it will take to pay you for this? Never mind, you black wench! we'll have a settlement when we get home. And as to these brats of yours, I've sold them to a man who will take them far enough out of your way; and as to this nigger, your adorable husband, his master has long been itching to give him a thousand lashes."

By this time Malvin was between the slave-hunters and their guns, and had his hand on his revolver. The parson was also in a suitable position, and ready for action.

"Get up here and be tied, you scoundrel," said Tom Bolton to Simon, at the same time kicking him.

Like lightning, the latter sprang to his feet, and, drawing back, struck the insolent wretch a blow that felled him like a dead man; and, before the other recovered from his surprise, he knocked him down, also.

The first one scrambled up and made for his gun; but, to his astonishment again, he found a pistol pointing at his breast, accompanied with the command to cross his hands and be tied.

In a few seconds, they were both tied with the same rope they had brought to tie poor Hannah with; and Simon had the satisfaction of tying one, and Hannah the other.

"Now, Hannah," said Parson Elmore, "you have a horse to ride to your new home in Kansas; and your husband will have two elegant farm-horses to drive business after you get there. But what will these nice young men do for spending-money, for egg-nog, oyster-suppers, mint-juleps, &c., when they no longer get your wages?"

This was too much for Tom Bolton; his chivalric blood boiled over. Never was any living animal seen to go into such a diabolical rage. He swore, stamped, and raved, pitched and tore, tried to break the rope with which he was bound, gnashed his teeth, and foamed at the mouth like a hard-ridden steed.

Hannah had noticed, when Tom first came up, that, besides his gun, he carried in his hand a keen, long, wiry hickory, something like an ox-goad; and she made no doubt that he had selected it in his rambles through the wilds for her special benefit. While the fellow was yet raving, she chanced to put her eye on this nicely-trimmed rod; and, obeying an impulse which suddenly awoke in her bosom, from a vivid recollection which flashed across her mind, of the deep wrongs she had suffered at the hands of the beast who was then raging because of being foiled in his Satanic purpose of venting his malice upon her, she snatched up the rod, and, flying at him like an enraged tigress, made the welkin ring with the sharp, keen lashes she laid on his back. Malvin and Parson Elmore thought the rascal deserved a flogging, and that, if anybody had a special right to administer it to him, it was Hannah; so they said nothing. And as for Simon, he enjoyed the scene immeasurably.

The hickory-storm that so unexpectedly burst upon the villain's back and shoulders surprised and confounded him to such a degree that he instantly gave up his raving, and stood stock-still, as if transfixed to the earth.

After linting him keenly for a few moments, Hannah paused, and, looking the guilty wretch in the eye, asked him if he remembered tying her, as he was then tied, and cutting her back to pieces with a cowhide, and for no other offence than having gone, without liberty, to see her husband, whom she had not seen for months. "And do you recollect," said she, "how you used to beat me when I failed to finish the heavy tasks you put upon me? You have never known before what it was to be lashed like a slave. Can you blame me for giving you a little taste of the sweets of slavery?"

Tom could make no reply, but stood in sullen

silence; yet plainly showed that the Devil was in him, big as a bull-dog.

"Slaves always have to beg before they are spared," continued Hannah; "and many times that doesn't save them till they are almost killed. And now, you miserable sinner, I'll teach you what it is to beg." And, stepping back and taking hold of the rod with both hands, she made it fairly talk round his shoulders. At first, he thought to grin and bear it; but the agony was too great; the unfeeling tyrant had to beg,—ay, to beg at the feet of a slave,—to ask mercy of one to whom he had shown no mercy! This was, indeed, humiliating for a slave-driving tyrant; but the smart of the lash soon brought down his lofty air, his arrogant looks, and inflated self-esteem. Having humbled him to her satisfaction, Hannah threw down the rod and turned away, saying, "Tom, I hope this lesson will profit you all your life, and teach you at least to feel for others."

The party now made preparations to travel on. It was deemed expedient to take the slave-hunters with them a day's journey or more, lest they should hurry home and put the guerrilla bands on their track.

Hannah and her children were mounted on Tom Bolton's big, strong horse, but now no longer his. Parson Elmore mounted the other horse, with their luggage, leaving Malvin and Simon to bring the prisoners on foot.

About noon, the day following, the parson thought it safe to turn the prisoners loose; so, calling a halt, Malvin divided with them a venison he had killed on the way with one of their guns; after which, the parson gave them a good piece of advice, to which they listened with sad looks, and then bade them farewell.

The next day, just before sundown, the party safely arrived at Simon's cabin in Kansas.

The reader can better imagine, than I can describe, the joy of Hannah and her husband when they came fully to realize that they were forever free from the shackles of slavery, and had a home on Freedom's soil.

10

CHAPTER VIII.

"Thus may we gather honey from the weed,
And make a moral of the Devil himself."

IN answer to the prayers, earnest entreaties, and pressing importunities, of many loyal citizens of Missouri, the Federal Government, after long delays, and the most tardy movements, as it seemed, of the War Department, at last sent forward into certain northern sections of the State, detachments of Union troops to assist Union men in maintaining the laws, and putting down mob-violence. The first Federal forces that made their appearance in Border-ruffian Rebeldom were altogether insufficient, and could afford very little protection either to the lives or property of the loyal party. Secessionists continued to maltreat, and, in many instances, murder their Union-loving neighbors. But the Federal forces at length began to be strengthened, and seriously to threaten the armed bands of reckless rebels that had broken up the peace of the country and inaugurated a reign of terror.

This menace created no little stir among secessionists; they lustily cried out, "*Invasion.*" And, wiping their mouths most sanctimoniously with their blood-stained hands and putting on a make-believe face and a lamb-like tone of innocence, appealed to the world, whether it was not a sin and a shame that a country, filled with such immaculate and unoffending people, should be invaded by government troops? And this hypocritical cry of *invasion* was echoed by the tories of the North from State to State, and from precinct to precinct. Yes; the willing tools of a Southern oligarchy caught this deceitful cry, fresh from the lips of perjured rebels and assassins, and have kept it resounding in disloyal sections of the Free States ever since.

Thus encouraged by hosts of copperheads at the North, the traitors of the southwest, especially of Missouri, made great noise of preparation for war. They met almost daily in great crowds to listen to their stump-orators, and lying demagogues, and to muster and drill, to drink whiskey, wrangle, and carouse.   Platte City was often the scene of these tumultuous gatherings and grand carousals.   The most notable assemblage of this sort took place there directly after the first Federal troops made their appearance at St. Joseph, some forty miles north of Platte City.   The whole country had been invited to turn out, for the purpose of raising a secesh flag, and of more effectually organizing and equipping a rebel force, to meet and vanquish the Union army.

The demagogues and nabobs were brave in words, but had no intention of being valorous in deeds ; it was well understood among them that the white trash were to do the fighting, while they did the talking, vaunting, and blowing of trumpets.

On the occasion alluded to above, Platte City was crowded to overflowing at an early hour, and all the ragamuffins of the land were on hand for a new suit of butternut, which, it was expected, the wealthy slave-holders would furnish, in view of the military services they were ready to render.

In the midst of the excitement, the attention of the multitude was all at once arrested by the sudden and imposing appearance of a coach and four coming down Main Street. The horses were richly caparisoned, and gayly bedecked about the ears with little flaunting banners, displaying the stars and bars, which had recently been substituted for the " rattlesnake flag,"— the first chosen ensign of the Southern Confederacy. A well-dressed negro, whose sable skin glistened like a newly-polished boot, sat pompously perched upon the box, reining, with more than princely pride, his prancing steeds, whose gorgeous trappings dazzled all eyes. Sambo flourished a new and superb whip, with a snapper on the end of the lash, which ever and anon he made pop like a pocket-pistol. This was according to the instructions of his master, who deemed it a modest way of announcing his advent, and was certainly less ostentatious than sounding a trumpet before him.

10*

"There comes Dr. Puff!" was whispered with enthusiasm in various groups.

"Dr. Puff! Dr. Puff!" went from lip to lip, and echoed from mouth to mouth through the restless, stirring multitude, as the glittering vehicle rolled by.

Driving on to the most fashionable inn, the ebony postilion pulled up; and a portly-bellied landlord waddled forth, and, opening the carriage-door, assisted a bloated specimen of humanity, like himself, to roll out.

One might have thought Jack Falstaff had again come to life, and was expecting a jolly greeting from "The Merry Wives of Windsor." On the obsequious crowd that gathered round, the nabob smiled a broad grin, and even deigned to shake by the hand, not only the upper ten, but also the lower million. To his white menials, and wealth-worshipping minions, this seemed a wondrous condescension.

Dr. Puff, though less burdened with brains than with some other things, well knew that in such times of commotion, the groundlings, and the low of station, had a chance for sudden ele-

vation. He saw that His Majesty, the mob,
already ruled the land ; and deemed it, therefore, expedient that he should due homage pay
to the populace. Men, whom he had never
stooped to greet before, were now in ecstasies
because the man of wealth deigned them the
notice of his eye. Little did their dull brains
perceive the inward thought of his scheming
mind, while he said within his heart, —

"These human cattle, during the coming
struggle, are to form the ramparts, behind which
we aristocrats, with our slaves, are to hide ourselves."

The excitement among the rabble, occasioned
by Dr. Puff's arrival, had scarcely subsided, when
another nabob rolled up in similar style, and to
whom all attention was at once turned.

Now Mr. Skedaddle had his day, and, for a
time, was the lion in his turn.

Being the largest slave-holder in that part of
the State, and of course interested in the slave-
holders' rebellion, and disposed to help it on
with his purse, his arrival produced a sensation
amounting to a furor ; and the glory which, but

a moment before, hovered around Dr. Puff, was at once totally eclipsed by the new celebrity, to the infinite mortification of the doctor.

The presence of these distinguished civilians on the occasion was well-calculated to promote the cause of secession, bolster treason, and give countenance to the rebellion; not, however, because of possessing either mental force or moral worth, for these celebrities could boast of neither; yet they had what was better, in the estimation of the vulgar herd, — money and slaves.

Dr. Puff, warm in the cause of disunion, and anxious to see sufficient means raised to arm and equip the rabble, felt inclined to urge upon his wealthy friend, Mr. Skedaddle, whom he thought rather penurious, to give largely in support of the enterprise; so he signified to the latter, as soon as an opportunity presented, his wish to speak with him aside. They walked off out of the bustle a few rods, and paused for conversation.

In personal appearance the two aristocrats presented a striking contrast. Skedaddle was lean and slender, nervous and excitable, and only lacked brain to be a man of thought and discernment. Dr. Puff was corpulent, lymphatic, tardy in his movements, and slow of speech. Like an elephant, he was hard to excite, but, when once fairly aroused, moved like a steam-engine, and, if angry, grew ferocious. He was especially capable of being wrought up to a high pitch of excitement upon any question affecting the safety of the *peculiar institution.*

Though very dissimilar in almost every respect, yet these swell-head rebels, at one point, were alike. They each attached great importance to the aristocracy of wealth, while mental and moral culture, wisdom and learning, had little or no value in their estimation. Like most ignorant men, they were full of vain conceit, and piqued themselves greatly upon their aristocracy; yet certain vulgar habits perpetually betrayed their low breeding.

Dr. Puff had the very odious habit of enforcing his remarks, whenever he made a point, by a chuck with his elbow into the short ribs of his listener, while Skedaddle had acquired the scarcely less disagreeable habit of echoing the last words of the individual in conversation with him, and, also, of forever repeating a couple of stereotyped exclamations. At every little surprise he would cry out, "*Remarkable!*" with a peculiar stress of voice; and, at every declaration made by his companion, he would exclaim, with great emphasis, "*Just so!*"

With this brief description of the two most wealthy aristocrats in Border-ruffian Rebeldom, I proceed to relate their private conversation.

After a very emphatic gesture, accompanied with a special effort to look wise, Dr. Puff thus began:—

"Now, Mr. Skedaddle,"—

"Just so, Dr. Puff," responded his nervous friend, anticipating him.

"You and I,"—

"Just so!"

At this juncture a loud hurrah was heard up street.

"Remarkable!" exclaimed Skedaddle, wheeling quickly round, and looking wildly in the direction of the shouting multitude.

" 'Tis but the parading of the rabble," explained Dr. Puff.

"Just so! the parading of the rabble," iterated the excited man, turning again, with a
patronizing air, to his confidential friend.

"I say *rabble;* perhaps I should say, *citizens,*"
remarked the doctor with a knowing wink, and,
at the same time, chucking Skedaddle with his
elbow in the side.

"Remarkable!" cried the lean-ribbed nabob,
jumping almost out of his boots; but in a moment recovered himself, and, affecting the utmost composure, replied, "Just so, citizens!"

Now came hurrying on, amid loud huzzas
and the stirring drum, a grand procession of
flaunting banners and ragged ruffians, with here
and there a decent-looking man, whose eye
seemed to say, "*I'm in for bunkum.*"

The procession was led by Mr. Scallawag, who
carried a secesh flag, and ever and anon broke
forth in a two-line song : —

> " Under the stars and bars,
> We're going to the wars — Oho !"

"Hurrah! hurrah! hurrah!" shouted the mob, waving hats and caps, or wildly flinging them high in air.

"Remarkable!" cried Mr. Skedaddle.

Next came Knickerbocker, with a wink and a blink, waving his hat in mock gesture; and then, in a stentorian voice, sang the following lines:—

> "I swear by the great Palmetto Nation,
>   We'll lick the Yankees like all tarnation!"

Then, suddenly dropping his voice into an undertone, added, "In a horn!"

"Hurrah! hurrah!" again shouted the rabble.

"Remarkable!" still exclaimed the excitable Skedaddle.

As soon as the noisy tumult had passed by, Dr. Puff resumed the conversation.

"As I was about to say, Mr. Skedaddle," —

"Just so!"

"You and I have property, and that property consists mainly in niggers."

"Just so! mainly in niggers."

"And niggers, you know, have legs;" at the same time chucking him in the ribs.

"Remarkable!" squalled the persecuted Skedaddle, jumping up and springing round like a
jaybird on a swinging limb. But directly check-
ing himself up, said, —

"Just so! niggers have legs."

"And the black rascals only want a chance to
use them," added Dr. Puff.

"Just so! a chance to use them."·

"Then only think what might happen to you
and me if the Lincoln troops are allowed to in-
vade Missouri; first thing we know," —

"Just so! first thing we know," —

"We'll be left niggerless!" again hunching
him.

"Remarkable!" bellowed Skedaddle, whirling
round, and clapping his hand on his side as if
feeling for a broken rib; then, again, as before,
suddenly calming down, reiterates the last words
of the imperturbable Dr. Puff, "just so!—left
niggerless!"

"And what a fix that would be for aristocrats
like you and me!"

"Just so!—aristocrats like you and me."

"Brought down upon a level with every poor

white devil, who is now glad to be our menial!"

"Just so!—glad to be our menial."

"Only look at it, sir; such a thought is ab-
solutely startling!"

Simultaneously with the utterance of the word
startling, he planted his ill-mannered elbow with
startling emphasis, yet all-unconscious of what
he did, about the tender region of the poor fellow's fifth rib.

"Remarkable!" bawled Skedaddle, as if he'd
been stabbed with a bowie-knife. But as soon as
he recovered his breath, he smothered his wrath,
and graciously sent back the echo,—"Just so!
—startling!"

"You and I well understand what it is that
keeps the *upper ten* above the *lower million!*"

"Just so! the *upper ten* above the *lower million!*"

"In *this* country it's *niggers* that lifts a man
up!" With the word *up,* went another dig of
the elbow into the dominion of ribs.

"Remarkable!—Plague take his elbow! That's
enough to lift a man *up* out of his boots," solilo-

quized Skedaddle with almost exhausted patience. But, perceiving that his friend was wholly unconscious of the pain and annoyance it gave him, he concluded to put on fortitude and bear it.

"Just so! It's *niggers* that lifts a man up."

"And the want of niggers lets him down."

"Just so! lets him down!"

"How would you feel, sir, aristocrat as you are, to have a *poor* man come along-side of you, and, presuming himself your equal, chuck you in the ribs, as I do?" And again the everlasting elbow came in collision with lean ribs.

"Remarkable! May Old Ringtail fancy me if I like to have any man punch me in the ribs at such a rate, — rich or poor!" These side-remarks of poor, tormented Skedaddle were not all uttered in an undertone; they only went unheeded by Dr. Puff, on account of his being so absorbingly occupied with what he himself was saying.

"Now, Mr. Skedaddle," remarked the doctor, with great earnestness, "you and I, and all Missouri slave-holders, will find it to our interest to lean to the South and kick against the North."

"Just so! to lean to the South and kick against the North."

"But to come at once to the point, Mr. Skedaddle, let me tell you, sir, we've got to fight;" said Dr. Puff, laying particular stress on the last word, and the usual emphasis on the poor fellow's ribs.

"Remarkable! Just so! No, no! Fight? Not while my name's Skedaddle!" And, wheeling about, began to make off.

"Hold! hold! I pray you, hold, sir," cried Dr. Puff; "let me explain."

Pausing as if to reflect, Skedaddle said to himself, —

"When I'm fool enough to knock my head against cold lead, may I be shot!"

"Your pardon, sir; you comprehend me not. I mean we must see that fighting's done."

"Just so! Oh, ho! see that fighting's done!" said the cowardly nabob, brightening up, and coming back.

"Pray, sir, what have you and I to dread? Aristocrat blood ne'er was made to be shed."

"Just so! ne'er was made to be shed."

"Of danger *we'll* be well aware. Sure there's *plebeian blood* to spare."

"Just so, plebeian blood to spare."

"Now, as to fighting, you know, 'tis easy to make some show, and, at the same time, manage to keep ourselves out of harm's way."

"Just so! out of harm's way."

"This, then, I only need suggest, — while we are sparing of our *blood*, we must be lavish of our *cash*. It may cost us a nigger or two, but what of that?"

"Just so! what of that?"

"Ah, ha! they are already hoisting the Confederate flag. Let us go mix in, shout, and wave our hats for bunkum!" And, with the inflection of the voice on the word *bunkum*, the doctor's impertinent elbow again took his martyred listener in the short ribs.

"Remarkable!" cried Skedaddle; "my ribs should be made of iron!" Then, turning to follow the doctor, who had already put his ponderous body in motion, said, — "Just so! go mix in, shout, and wave our hats for bunkum!"

CHAPTER IX.

"The best laid plans o' mice and me
Gang aft agley."

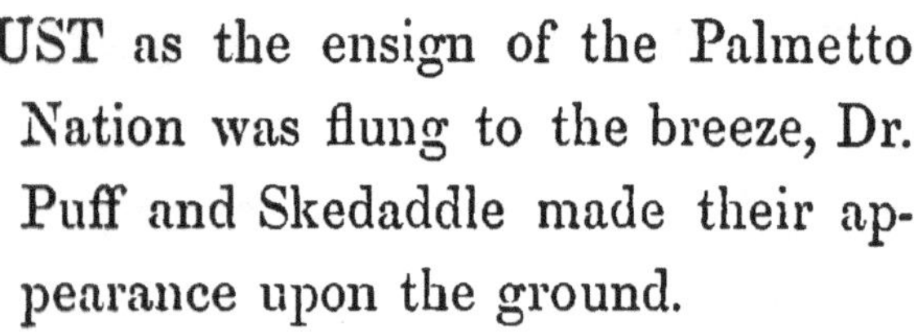

UST as the ensign of the Palmetto Nation was flung to the breeze, Dr. Puff and Skedaddle made their appearance upon the ground.

"Hail to the stars and bars!" cried Dr. Puff, waving his hat with great enthusiasm.

"Just so! hail to the stars and bars!" echoed Skedaddle, flourishing his hat in like manner.

"Three cheers for Jeff. Davis, Beauregard, and the Southern Confederacy!" shouted a guerrilla chief.

"The Devil's trinity!" added Knickerbocker, aside.

"Hurrah! hurrah! hurrah!" went up from the rabble. At which, Skedaddle said, "Remarkable!"

At this juncture, two very genteel-looking men came up, stopping on the outskirts of the tatterdemalion crowd.

"Just listen to these infernal rebels!" said one to the other.

"Again!" shouted the guerrilla chief, waving his hat. The multitude followed, and a second loud hurrah went up for the stars and bars.

"Perdition overtake them!" said one of the two outside gentlemen just alluded to.

"A vile clan!" responded his companion.

"I could see every rascal of them swing upon a limb!" remarked the former; "what say you, Mr. Rupert?"

"Ah, let them yell!" was the indifferent response; "empty heads will be loud-mouthed."

"Again!" shouted the guerrilla chief; and now a third wild hurrah rent the air around the rebel flag.

The excited gentleman outside the tumult still grew warmer. "Confound the gallows-looking traitors!" said he; "how well their necks would become halters!"

"I pray you keep cool, Mr. Haller."

"Leave these blockheads to the foolkiller," rejoined his companion.

"Perhaps them demure-looking gentlemen in white shirts don't like it," observed a leading demagogue, looking toward Rupert and Haller.

"By their looks they seem to say so," remarked Knickerbocker, putting on a make-believe face.

"Who cares?" growled the demagogue; "they'd better make tracks if they don't want a shower of brickbats."

"I trust the hangman may soon find employment, and we market for our hemp," observed Haller to Rupert, as they turned about to withdraw.

"Three groans for the old stars and stripes!" said the guerrilla chief, at the top of his voice.

"And three times three for yourselves, poor devils," rejoined Knickerbocker, aside.

Three hideous groans were straightway given in response to the chief's request. At the end of each groan, Skedaddle solemnly uttered his oft-repeated exclamation, "Remarkable!"

In the midst of this farcical scene, a man came running down the street in breathless haste, crying, at the top of his voice, "The Federals! the Federals! the Federals!"

"Remarkable!" exclaimed Skedaddle, taking a flying attitude.

"Heaven save us!" cried Knickerbocker, affecting great consternation. "We're gone up," added he; "pull the flag down."

"Just so!" said Skedaddle, starting to run; "pull the flag down."

Great confusion ensued, which directly became a general stampede. Helter-skelter they went, the cowardly renegades flying in every direction, and hiding themselves in every conceivable place.

An Irishman, who just came upon the ground in time to witness the flight of the panic-stricken rabble, and who had learned that it was a false alarm, cried out, —

"St. Pater! what ligs they've goot! Brave min! they outroon the wind! Coom bock! coom bock, ivery frightened divil of ye! There's niver a bit o' truth in what they say!

"By jabers! ond ait's mysilf thot wouldn't roon leik thot af all the divils in the pit were at my hales! Proper stoof for sooldiers! the viery oold boy couldn't kitch them!"

Dr. Puff, having run himself out of breath, finally undertook to hide behind a tree which was too small, by half, to conceal his enormous bulk; his waistband showed conspicuously on either side of it. "Heavens!" said he, in his perplexity; "I wish this tree were larger, or else myself were gaunter. Surely, my dimensions never were so great before!"

It soon became known that the stampede was caused by a false alarm; and the dismayed and scattered chivalry, one by one, began to return.

Knickerbocker, who had but little exhausted himself in flight, was the first to get back.

"A weak invention of the enemy," said he to Patrick, the Irishman, with great seeming mortification.

"May the Divil take the waked sinner that meiks a brave mon show the white fither," said Patrick, with a leer.

"Upon my word, Pat," remarked Knickerbocker, with apparent seriousness, "I cannot help having a secret admiration for the Irish soldier who saved his life by buckling his breast-plate on behind."

"Faith! ond thot Irishmon moost o' been boorn in Amiriky."

Now back came Dr. Puff and Mr. Skedaddle; the latter, looking somewhat chop-fallen, said, "Remarkable!"

"A Black Republican fabrication!" exclaimed the former, ill-naturedly.

"And only meant for our vexation," chimed in Knickerbocker.

"By jabers! I seed 'em mysilf," said Pat; "bad luck to them! but not Fiderals, — our own min they were; ond rigular jay-hookers!"

"Is that so, Patrick?" demanded Dr. Puff.

"Sure's the Divil's a sinner, yer honor," answered Pat, with great earnestness.

"Why, in the deuce, did we run?" muttered the doctor, half-audibly, and as if out of humor with himself for betraying such cowardice.

"Faith! ond yer honest ligs wouldn't stand; and aisn't that rason enoof?" Then, to himself,

said, " Sooldiers are made of daferent stoof.
Upon my sowl, thase blusterin' rebels brag and
roon, roon and brag. 'Taise a tight race 'twaixt
ligs ond toongue; the viry Divil can't till
whaich'll wun ! "

Dr. Puff, anxious to put the best possible face
on the disgraceful affair, looked up at the flag,
and, waving his hat, said, —

" Wave on, gallant banner, wave ! "

" Wave over the sons of the brave ! " added
Knickerbocker, in an ironical tone, and waving
his hat with mock gesture.

" Just so ! " said Skedaddle; " over the sons of
the brave ! "

Patrick thought it was time for him to chime
in; so, taking off his torn and tattered beaver
and waving it in circles round his head,
shouted, —

" Long lave Master Skedaddle ! waith a joomp
ond a spraddle he daistanced the foe ! "

" Plague take the Irishman ! " said Dr. Puff,
aside, to Skedaddle; " he's impudent."

" Just so ! — impudent."

The day was spent, as many others had been before it, in noise and bustle, empty words and vaporing, and ended in a general spree, all going home drunk.

12

CHAPTER X.

"Firm in his loyalty he stood,
And prompt to seal it with his blood."

THERE resided in the country, a short distance from Platte City, an old citizen of Missouri, whom the secessionists had sought hard to win over to their disloyal cause on account of his wealth and influence. He was a man of few words, but of sound judgment, wisdom, and discretion. Attentive to his own business, he had kept himself at home, avoiding crowds, town-meetings, and all scenes of tumult and excitement, until the work of violence, house-burning, robbery, and assassination had commenced in terrible earnest.

His first step in taking an open stand against secession was to hang out the star-spangled banner over his own door. The flag was a magnificent one, — ample in its folds, of finest tissue, and surmounted by a large eagle; and also a beautiful picture of the Goddess of Liberty putting her foot upon the head of a coiled rattlesnake.

A few days after it was flung to the breeze, a band of armed ruffians made their appearance at the old man's gate.

"Mr. Marlow," said the captain of the company, "what means this display of the old Yankee flag?"

"Who taught you, sir, thus to stigmatize our nation's ensign, — the glorious old flag of the Union?" responded the patriot.

"No matter," returned the captain; "it must straightway come down."

"Be not too positive."

"My orders must be promptly obeyed."

"Your words and manner have too much of the crack of the overseer's whip; from being accustomed, perhaps, to giving orders at negro quarters. If I mistake not, you were a hireling in that business before you entered upon your present occupation of jay-hawking."

"I've neither time nor patience to argue with any Black Republican. The decree has gone forth that the old stars and stripes can no longer float over Missouri soil."

"Heaven grant I may not live to see that day!"

"If your prayer is answered, 'tis time your grave was dug."

The old patriot, lifting his eyes to the banner, and gazing upon it in silence for a few moments as it floated gracefully upon the breeze, said, —

"I love that flag, — that good old flag, — and have entwined each thread of the glorious tissue about my heart-strings."

"I'd much rather hear of some hemp being entwined round your neck, you infernal abolitionist!" muttered one of the ruffians.

"Hemp is for the necks of traitors," retorted Marlow, calmly; and, looking up again at the flag, said, "The stars and stripes have floated over my cradle, and it is my prayer that they may float over my grave."

"You'd better die, then, in some other country than this," answered the captain, morosely.

" It matters little where, so I but fill a patriot's grave," returned Marlow, calmly.

" You've heard my orders; take down the flag."

" That banner, sirs," said the old man, with deep feeling, and with spontaneous and impressive eloquence, " is, in my eyes, an emblem of all that is grand in human history, and of all that is transporting in human hope. And if it is to be sacrificed on the altars of a Satanic ambition, and disappear forever amid the night and tempest of revolution, then may I feel that the sun has been stricken from the sky of my life; and that henceforth I am to be but a wanderer and an outcast, with nought but the bread of sorrow and of penury for my lips, and with hands ever outstretched in feebleness and supplication, on which, in any hour, a military tyrant may rivet the fetters of a despairing bondage. May God, in his infinite mercy, save you and me, and the land we so much love, from such a degradation!"

" Our business is to see that this flag is taken down," said the captain, impatiently, and in a tone of anger.

12*.

"I want us to gaze upon that flag, that peradventure we may catch the spirit that breathes upon us from the battle-fields of our fathers. I am resolved that, come weal or woe, I will, in life and in death, now and forever, stand by the stars and stripes."

"Then must you leave the State of Missouri, and follow that emblem of Black Republicanism in some other part of the earth."

"This country is my home, and the home of those who are near and dear to me. Here our children were born, and here is our all; and here have we the right to remain unmolested."

"Not if you're opposed to secession."

"As free men, we are wont to boast of civil and religious liberty; and we have gloried in the freedom of speech, and in the freedom of the press. Can we any longer glory in these, or boast that ours is a land of freedom, if we are disallowed to speak freely our political opinions, and disallowed to sit beneath the ensign that our fathers were proud of, and which all nations respect? Great God! has it come to this, that our country, that liberty, rights of conscience, and everything sacred, is to be sacrificed to the institution of slavery?"

"We've heard enough. That flag must come down."

"And are you Americans? the sons of sires who, in 'the days that tried men's souls,' followed the stars and stripes over ensanguined fields, and through many a storm of leaden hail where fierce battle raged? The descendants of patriots who helped plant the tree of liberty, and who watered it with their blood, can you find it in your hearts to pull down and trample upon that flag? Can you dishonor our country's banner,—that banner which has been unfurled from the snows of Canada to the plains of New Orleans, and to the halls of the Montezumas, and amid the solitudes of every sea? And everywhere, as the luminous symbol of resistless and beneficent power, it has led the brave and the free to victory and to glory!"

"We'll hear no more. Take down the accursed flag!"

"*I* take down that flag? No, never! It has been my fortune to look upon the stars and stripes in foreign lands, and amid the gloom of an Oriental despotism, and right well do I know, by contrast, how bright are those stars, and how sublime are their inspirations! I cannot take down that glorious banner."

"Then we will do it for you," said the captain, advancing with drawn sword, and followed by his men.

"Not while I am able to defend it," said the brave patriot, presenting a pistol. "Back! villains, back! Traitors, emissaries of hell, avaunt!"

The audacious miscreants beat a hasty retreat. When fairly out of harm's way, they halted to look back, and just in time to hear the patriot's apostrophe to the waving stars and stripes.

"Float on, my country's banner! no coward hand shall grapple, nor traitor fingers defile or trail thee in the dust, while I have an arm to strike and a soul to dare."

"Upon my word, there's danger in the fellow," said the captain; "perhaps we'd better let him alone for the present."

"So I think," said a subaltern, " and take him on surprise some dark night when he's asleep."

This was agreed upon, and the wretches left the loyal man's premises, but with deadly malice in their hearts, and determined on revenge at no distant day.

CHAPTER XI.

" Thy head at price, thy steps waylaid."

THE day following the affair related in the preceding chapter, Mr. Rupert, a Union man of Platte City, hastened to the house of Mr. Marlow, and, in a fever of excitement, said to the brave patriot, —

"My friend, I am alarmed for your safety. Men are losing their senses; the secession fever is raging; the whole country's in a passion; rapine and murder have come to be the order of the day. Believe me, we cannot breast the storm, and had as well give it up."

"Give it up?" replied Marlow, — "and what then?"

"Why, if need be, float with the tide, at least, till the excitement's over."

"I know the peril," responded the patriot, "and I know my duty too. Dark is the hour; the howl of the storm is in our ears, and the lightning's red glare is painting terror on the sky. But all the more imperious is our call to duty."

"At such a time, what can we do? Law and order are set aside, and a reign of terror is now inaugurated."

"Can we be idle spectators of the scene, while the ship of State pitches and rolls under the lashings of the waves, and is in constant danger of going down?"

"Ah, but I entreat you, consider the terrible crisis through which we are passing, and the reckless determination of the revolutionists. To oppose them is to be overwhelmed. Deliberately ask yourself what course wisdom and prudence would dictate under such fearful circumstances."

"That have I already done. Besides, I've considered the machinations by which this national tragedy has been brought upon us. And, when I look upon this bright land, a few months since so prosperous, so tranquil, and now behold it plunged into a state of anarchy, conflict, and bloody strife, and being darkened and desolated, and the hearts of millions bleeding and wrung with anguish, and know, as I do, that all this is the work of a score or two of men, who, over all this national ruin and despair, are preparing to carve with the sword their way to seats of permanent power, I cannot but feel an irrepressible and burning indignation; and that I have a duty to perform in opposing their wicked scheme."

"I grant you, the authors of our great trouble will have much to answer for."

"Ah, they are accumulating upon their souls an amount of guilt hardly equalled in all the atrocities of treason and of homicide that have degraded the annals of our race from the foundations of the world."

"But pray, what can you and I do by opposing the madness of the people? Or what can all the Union men in the community accomplish? Men have lost their reason, and are being transformed to brutish beasts. And in vain may we appeal to the understandings or the consciences of the excited populace; they have had a taste of blood, and, like tigers, they rage and are mad for more."

" 'Tis even so. But forget not that among the most powerful instrumentalities relied on for reëstablishing the authority of the government, is that of the Union sentiment of the South, sustained by a liberated press. It is now trodden to the earth, but rest assured we shall not long be left to battle alone against the mob; the Federal Government will send us aid; then will loyal men, in dark sections like this, begin to look their oppressors in the face."

" Ah, but we may yet see it here, as it now is in the seceded States; there, no man expresses an opinion opposed to the revolution but at the imminent hazard of life and property. The only light which is admitted into political discussion is that which flashes from the sword or gleams from glistening bayonets. And secessionists are doing all that within them lies to bring on the same state of things in Missouri."

" I trust a darkness so deep, dismal, and impervious will never gather over us. The ordeal through which we are passing, doubtless, will involve immense suffering and losses for us all; but the expenditure, however great, will be well made if the result shall be the preservation of our institutions."

" That I admit, but certainly the result is dubious. Think of the fearful odds against which we must contend if the Federal Government delays sending us help."

" Let us not despair that help will come. No contest so momentous as this has ever before arisen in human history; for, amid all the conflicts of men and nations, the existence of no such a government as ours has ever been at stake."

" True, most true."

" Our fathers won our independence by the blood and sacrifice of a seven-years' war; and we have maintained it against the assaults of the greatest power upon the earth ; and the question now is, whether we are to perish by our own hands, and have the epitaph of *suicide* written ıpon our tomb !"

" The force of your argument I grant; but the perplexing question still returns, What can we do?"

" Be not troubled about that; we can all do something in this noble struggle."

" I see not how."

" It is a contest between right and wrong; between loyal men and traitors, and between freedom and slavery. A great work is to be done, and each one of us can take a part. The remorseless agitators at the South, who made the revolution, and now hold its reins, must be discarded alike from the public confidence and the public service. The country, in its agony, is feeling their power; and, although it may be difficult to overthrow the ascendancy they have secured, yet it must be done."

" But can they be overthrown ?"

" If the Union men of the Slave States would but rise up with one accord, they'd find themselves fully equal to the emergency."

" Uncertain. Treason has its emissaries, and the rebellion its secret agents, going forth night and day, lighting the fires, and fanning the flames of civil war."

"Let such emissaries and agitators perish politically and forever. 'A breath can unmake them as a breath has made;' but destroy this Republic, and, 'where is that promethean art that can its light relume?' Once entombed, when will the angel of the resurrection descend to the portals of its sepulchre? There's not a voice which comes to us from the cemetery of nations that does not answer, Never! never!"

"Said a great French statesman to an American citizen, a few months since, 'Your Republic is dead; and it is probably the last the world will ever see. You will have a reign of terror, and, after that, two or three monarchies.'"

"Should this revolution succeed, his words may be verified. But it must not succeed. There is loyalty enough in the land to arrest it; it surely will be arrested."

"Heaven grant it may," said Rupert; and took his departure without having accomplished the object of his visit.

Though undecided as to what might be the best policy, Rupert belonged not to that class of men who wavered between union and secession.

He had no temptation to espouse the rebel cause; but seemed to think himself justifiable in taking a neutral position for the sake of being more secure in person and property. This course, under some circumstances, was certainly justifiable. While a true patriot is ready and willing to make sacrifices, at the same time, he should place too much value on his life to hazard it when nothing beneficial to his country is likely to be achieved thereby. The most despicable class of men we had in Missouri were those who were ready to be bought and sold, and who, for money, would fight on either side. The majority of these unprincipled wretches ultimately went into guerrilla bands; professed to be the champions of Southern rights and defenders of the people, yet they would rob or murder friend or foe as interest or passion prompted.

In less than a fortnight from the time the band of ruffians went to Marlow's to take down the stars and stripes, the good old patriot was surprised at dead of night, dragged from his

18*

pillow, and assassinated in the presence of his wife and children.

After this bloody deed, — this most atrocious and savage murder,—the assassins drove out the surviving members of the family, without even giving them time to attire themselves decently, and then dismantled the house and set it on fire, — reducing to ashes what they could not carry off, — and, with the dwelling, consumed the body of their murdered victim.

CHAPTER XII.

" This is the crisis of my fate."

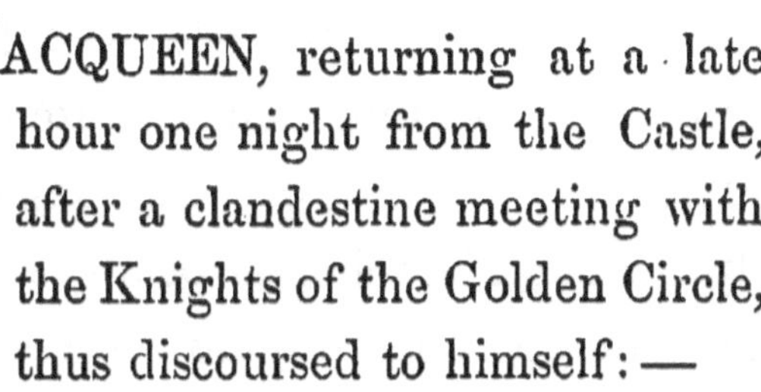MACQUEEN, returning at a late hour one night from the Castle, after a clandestine meeting with the Knights of the Golden Circle, thus discoursed to himself: —

"Why do I hesitate? The spice of danger but gives relish to great achievements, and sweetens the wine of success. Give me something to win, something to lose, else life grows tame, and its best joys stale.

"God has given me ambition; and for what, if not to climb, to shine, to soar?"

Macqueen, though by no means a good man, yet was far from being the worst man in the world. He possessed a nature that easily assimilated itself to surroundings, and readily took

on the moral tone and coloring of minds and
hearts with which he was brought into contact.
The good and the evil within him were alike
easily excited and brought into play. His conscience, though elastic, was not seared; frequently seized with qualms, it gave him much
trouble; consequently he was always sinning
and repenting. His wife, who had a powerful
influence over him, had repeatedly brought him
almost to the point of abandoning secession and
discarding his rebel associates; but as soon as
he came in contact again with vile traitors and
cunning, intriguing politicians, he was at once
imbued with their spirit and sentiments, and,
thereby, lost the more wholesome and salutary
influence which his wife had exerted upon him.
This frailty, together with an inordinate ambition for distinction, had much to do in making
him disloyal to his country. Besides this, being
a member of the Inner Temple of the Knights
of the Golden Circle, he was bound by treacherous and disloyal oaths to aid treason and promote the cause of secession. Yet his better nature frequently revolted at measures of cruelty

and injustice advocated in the Castle, and sometimes adopted by the Order.

On the occasion alluded to above, he had been promoted to the highest office in the Inner Temple, which vastly inflated his vanity, and spurred anew his vaulting ambition. When the Castle adjourned, which was sometime after midnight, he repaired homeward with his mind full of golden dreams and magnificent air-castles.

As the clock struck twelve, Mrs. Macqueen had risen from her sleepless pillow and seated herself at the window of her chamber to look on the waning moon and think about her absent husband.

"Oh, this is terrible!" exclaimed she, while conversing with her own heart. "My husband disloyal! the father of my children guilty of treason, and leagued with conspirators and the enemies of his country! Kind Heaven, how shall I endure it? Oh, what fiend could have put this madness into his brain?"

While these painful thoughts were revolving in her mind, and escaping her lips in words softly and sadly uttered, Macqueen entered her chamber, manifestly so occupied with his own imaginings as to be oblivious of everything else.

"How strange you have grown of late, Mr. Macqueen!" observed his wife, after waiting in vain for him to speak first.

"Strange,—how strange?" replied he, as if scarcely conscious of where he was or what he said.

"You look and act," said she, "like one asleep and dreaming strange dreams."

"Truly, I've been dreaming," returned he,—"have had a magnificent dream."

"I hope it was an honest dream," returned she.

"I only wish I could describe to you, my dear," said the husband, with animation, "the sparkling, gorgeous visions that have to-night been floating before my mind's eye in such dazzling splendor!—visions of thrones, crowns, and sceptres! visions of royalty,—of purple robes, flashing diamonds, and a brilliant retinue! ay, and a new race of nobles, princes, and princesses!"

"I sadly fear there's lunacy working on his brain," said his wife to herself, gazing upon him with anxiety and amazement.

"And I've been pondering," continued he, "the lessons of history,—ruminating upon what has been, and speculating on what might be. I've called to mind how ancient republics have fallen, and how from their ruins kingdoms, empires, and monarchies have risen up."

"On what vagaries he feeds his vain hope!" said Mrs. Macqueen, mentally, while the darkness of despair gathered about her heart.

"And, not all forgetful of my humble origin," he yet continued, "I've recounted instances in which intrepid, daring spirits have, from obscurity, suddenly emerged, and, bravely mounting up the slippery steeps of Fame, stood upon her very pinnacle!"

"What is all this harangue about?" demanded his wife; at the same time seizing hold of and shaking him violently, as if to rouse him from a deep sleep. "Wake up to your right senses!" cried she; "surely, you are going mad!"

"Mad!" echoed the husband, peevishly; "that's

just like a woman; you've no appreciation of my great ideas!"

"Like the sun-painted clouds of a summer evening, your gaudy visions will soon wear a leaden hue, fade, and disappear."

"Prophesy against me, if you will; nothing can change my purpose; I'm bent on mounting upward."

"Think not to take away the curse by making vile treachery and foul treason wear a gloss."

"Revolutions give opportunity to the aspiring, the ambitious, and men of great souls."

"Revolutions also give rare opportunities to knaves, who are ready to seize upon the misfortunes of their country to benefit themselves."

"Madam, you have no conception of my aspirations."

"Ah, lofty, I dare say; but I'll venture to guess just what they are: You anticipate the triumph of the slave-power, and imagine, when despotism is ready to distribute the rewards of treason, by putting sceptres into the hands of a swarm of petty kings, that you will find yourself on a throne. This is the length and breadth

of your ambition and the height of your tower-
ing aspirations. And this accounts for your
waking dream, which, I predict, will turn out
but the baseless fabric of a vision."

At a subsequent meeting of the Castle, Macqueen was deeply afflicted by a decree of the
Order, which sealed the fate of a young man,
who had left the fraternity and divulged some
of the secrets of the Inner Temple. He opposed the decree of death, but it was passed over
his head.

A committee of three were appointed to exe-
cute the bloody decree.

The offender resided a short distance in the
country, and the day following he walked into
town on an errand, just after nightfall, pur-
chased some goods, and, taking the bundle on
his shoulder, started immediately homeward.

The committee of assassins, being on the
alert, followed him. Leaving the main road,
the young man, to save distance, took a narrow
path, which led through a lonely grove. Thinking of no danger, and carrying a bundle on his
shoulder, he looked not back, but slowly walked

on, whistling all the while to keep himself company. In the midst of the solitary way, the assassin whose lot it was to strike the first blow might have been seen softly treading at his victim's heels, with a drawn dagger, which gleamed fearfully bright in the light of the moon.

Macqueen, whose conscience had been torturing him terribly, and whose mind had become almost frantic, thinking of the foul and bloody deed which he knew was in contemplation, had observed the assassins following the doomed man out of the village. Upon the impulse of the moment, he pencilled a line of warning, and, putting it into the hand of a slave, sent it after the young man; the servant was charged to make haste, and to deliver the note without a word of explanation, or telling who sent it. Unfortunately, the slave took the wrong road, and, going to the young man's home, gave the mysterious note to his father.

In the mean time, Macqueen, fearing the slave would fail to overtake the young man in time, had followed the parties himself, and with all possible speed ; and, but for losing his breath in making such haste, so as to be unable at once to speak, he would have saved the poor man's life. He had got in full view of the assassins and their victim, and in time to see the fatal blow struck. The murderers, seeing Macqueen coming, and not knowing who he was, immediately fled. On approaching the murdered man, who was just breathing his last breath, Macqueen so gave way to feelings of pity and remorse that he almost lost his reason. After gazing for a few moments with unspeakable agony upon the face of the dead man, he turned about and retraced his steps homeward, weeping as he went, and ever and anon incoherently talking to himself like a maniac. As he neared the village, he met the father of the unfortunate young man, hunting his son, and in great distress of mind, caused by the mysterious note he had received, which dimly hinted at assassination, but explained nothing satisfactorily. The fears of the disconsolate father were greatly increased when he discovered the frantic state of mind Macqueen was in.

After being plied with sundry questions, the

latter said, " My hands are unstained, but my tongue is tied. What I know I dare not reveal."

But after being much urged by the unhappy man to tell what he knew, he looked away, saying, —

> " I will talk into the air;
> What I say let no man hear."

Then in solemn tones he gave utterance to the following words : —

> " 'Twas on the road, the lonely road,
>   Under the still white moon, —
> Under the silent trees he strode.
>   He whistled and shifted his weary load, —
> He whistled a foolish tune.
>   Another's step timed with his own,
> A figure that stooped and bowed;
>   And a keen white blade that gleamed and shone
> Like a splinter of daylight downward thrown;
>   And the moon behind a cloud
> Then came out so broad and good,
>   The barn-fowl woke and crowed;
> He ruffled his feathers in drowsy mood,
> While the brown owl called out to his mate in the wood,
>   That a dead man lay in the road."

" Great God! they have murdered him!" exclaimed the old man, and at once hurried on in the direction which Macqueen mysteriously pointed, as he closed his strangely-told story.

The reader may be curious to know whether proper efforts were made to bring the assassins to justice. What would have been the use? Law was set aside, justice trampled under foot, and courts of judicature entirely set aside. Besides, nobody dared, at that time, to call to an account, for murder or any other crime, a Knight of the Golden Circle. Not only so, assassinations were so common that nobody was snrprised when a murder occurred; nor was it expected that the mnrderer would be brought to justice, unless some friend of the slain should take vengeance into his own hands, and shoot or stab the guilty wretch at an unexpected moment.

CHAPTER XIII.

"The wicked flee when no man pursueth."

THE reader must expect but a disjointed story, since the author is bound to confine his narrative mainly to the actual events that transpired around him, and at a period when the times were out of joint, and everything in a state of sad confusion and wild disorder. The characters already introduced are by no means dismissed; but, while following them, in their various careers, through troublous times and the fortunes of war, it is deemed proper and expedient to give some of the most prominent incidents and scenes, whether of a serious or ludicrous character, that happened in the interim.

In a work of imagination merely, the reader

has the right to expect a harmonious plot, a well-connected story, and a happy denouement; but, in a narrative of facts, no such thing can be reasonably looked for.

In the midst of our troubles in Missouri, we occasionally had something to laugh at, as well as a great deal to cry about.

In the latter part of the summer of '61, we had for our entertainment, every few days, more or less of tragi-comedy. Nothing could have been more comical, farcical, and ludicrous than some of our stampedes. And but for the terrible tragedies that were often enacted in such close connection with the stampedes, they would have set the whole world in a roar.

Rumors of the coming of Federal troops were perpetually on the wing for at least a fortnight before any were seen. And, during that time, the dashing of guerrilla bands to and fro over the country, who were not unfrequently mistaken, in the night-time, for Federal soldiers, caused frequent panics among secessionists.

To see a scared rebel — who had been fright-

ened out of his wits at sight of a dozen guerrillas, whom he had taken for a whole regiment
of Union troops—coming into town, under whip
and spur, with his hat off, and his hair and coat-
tail streaming wildly in the air, his face pale as
a ghost, and his eyes glaring like Macbeth's
when Banquo's bloody apparition shook his
gory locks at him,—and then to see him rise
in his stirrups, as he neared the village, and cry,
"Federals! Federals! Federals!" at the top
of his voice, to the no little danger of splitting
his throat,—was certainly ludicrous beyond the
power of language to describe.   And then to
see the villagers run,—breaking full speed in
every direction for the woods, the cornfields, and
hempfields,—even the most vivid imagination,
without having witnessed such a scene, cannot
conceive the laughable appearance it really has.
Oh that some great artist, some master painter,
had looked upon one of those scenes and made
a picture for future generations!

I will here attempt a brief description of the
seventh stampede we had at Platte City.

The busy tongue of report had somehow set

on foot the startling rumor, after many false alarms and needless flights, that a regiment of Union soldiers were really coming from St. Joseph, to take the town.

A rebel company of fifty men, called the Tigers, who made Platte City their headquarters, mounted their Mexican ponies, swearing vengeance against the Yankees, and set out, with great show of bravery, to meet and drive back the invaders.

Near the same time, another rebel company, called the Lions, who made New Market their rallying place, hearing the same report, seized their guns, mounted their horses, and started for Platte City, expecting there to join the Tigers, and make a stand against the Yankees.

Now New Market was twelve miles north of Platte City on the St. Joseph road; consequently, these companies had to meet somewhere on the way. Yet each squad was ignorant of the movements and intentions of the other.

About half-way between the places, the Lions and Tigers came in sight of one another.

The road being dry and the sun hot, an immense cloud of dust, of course, enveloped each squadron, which afforded a fine opportunity for the imagination to work; which easily magnified a small body of horsemen, dimly seen, into an army of gigantic proportions.

The Tigers, or Platte City Braves, as they were sometimes called, making sure they had met the enemy, wheeled quickly about, and, plunging their shanghai spurs into the sides of their ponies, made straight skirts and horizontal tails back toward Platte City.

The Lions, or New Market boys, had themselves pulled up, and were upon the point of flying, a moment before the Tigers took to their heels; but now, taking the hint who the other party were, and what had caused their panic, and well pleased to see the Tigers run, they concluded to follow on and make the most of the fun; so, plying whip and spur, they gave chase to the flying braves, who, the more terrified at finding themselves hotly pursued, at once threw their guns and every cumbrous thing to the winds, that, thus unencumbered, they might make the greater speed.

This so amused the Lions that they pressed on the faster, and directly raised a hideous yell that almost frightened the poor fugitives out of their wits.

Now, convinced that it was life or death, the panic-stricken Tigers resolved not to spare horse-flesh. Leaning forward, as if anxious to out-travel their scudding ponies, they plied, with might and main, their cruel heels to the reeking, gory flanks of their poor animals. So fast they went, the wind took off their hats and seemed seriously to threaten their streaming locks. Such a flight, spurred on by such fright, perhaps never before was seen.

While all this was transpiring, a large armed force of rebels, jay-hawkers, and guerrillas had gathered into Platte City, and were about following in the wake of the brave Tigers, to help drive back the invading Yankees. Before taking up their line of march, however, they deemed it expedient to call on John Barleycorn, prime their pans, and take a snort of red-eye.

About one-half of the army dismounted opposite the drinking-saloon, leaving the other

half to hold their horses, while they, with pitchers, pint-cups, and glass tumblers, passed round
the courage-inspiring beverage, — first to those
still in their saddles.

All the inhabitants of the town were out, of
course, to see and cheer the chivalrous defenders
of Southern rights.

Right in the midst of this oh-be-joyful scene,
as fortune would have it, the retreating Tigers,
in breathless haste, came tearing down the
dusty road, with the roaring Lions at their
heels.

The valorous chivalry before John Barleycorn's saloon, hearing the sudden clatter of a
hundred horses' feet, turned at once to look and
listen.

The commander-in-chief, seated on his stately
steed, feather in hat and sword by his side, had
just received from the hand of a subaltern a
brimming glass, which he held beneath his nose,
while he paused to gaze and wonder at what he
heard and saw.

The sparkling beverage, yet untasted, trem-
bled in his grasp. For once, though a drunkard,

he forgot to drink. His dilating eyes looked wildly out upon a huge cloud of dust, while his astonished ears drank in the startling chorus of loud-resounding hoofs, which swelled upon the circumambient air like the hoarse murmur of ocean's rolling billows, as nearer and more near the thunder sounded.

On, on, came the flying cavalcade, as if the very De'il was bringing up the rear.

Wildly, and more wildly the chieftain stared; nor did he stare alone: all stared, stared with all their eyes.

Now, while wonder and amazement stood tip-toe, a mighty cry arose amid the waving throng that crowded around John Barleycorn; and from lip to lip it flew: "*The tarnal Yankees are coming!*"

At this the chief grew deadly pale; the brimming cup fell from his palsied hand; and his unmoistened lips were heard to utter the ominous word,—"*Skedaddle!*"

What followed, gentle reader, you should have been there to see. Jingling glasses and broken pitchers made merry music on the rocky pavement.   And there was mounting in hot haste; nor did all get mounted ; riderless horses and horseless riders might have been seen scampering away in dire confusion.

In all the hurly-burly, nothing, perhaps, was more noticeable than the dexterity of a guerrilla chief, who, in his great haste to turn his back upon the advancing foe, as he supposed, mounted his war-horse, facing the wrong way, and, before discovering his mistake, spurred his charger, at the same time clutching at his tail for the bridle-rein.   By the time the poor fellow discovered his mistake, he found himself being carried backward, at full speed, into the very face of danger.

All in all, it was a scene, the like of which a man may not expect to look upon more than once in a lifetime.

It was a real tragi-comedy, and, though laughable, turned out altogether a disastrous stampede.   Frightened men and horses, sadly mixed, plunging and floundering, went helterskelter, running over white and black, big and little, men and women.

The town was soon cleared, except by the unfortunate creatures who were trampled under foot and too badly crippled to get away.

Scarcely was the village emptied of one set of frightened rebels when it was filled by another, no less terrified. As soldiers and citizens went out like a whirlwind at one end of the town, the dismayed Tigers and yelling Lions came in like an earthquake at the other.

The Tigers, finding their friends gone and the village deserted, concluded, in their despair, to surrender. Calling a halt, they gave themselves up to their pursuers, doubting not that they were falling into the hands of the merciless Yankees, of whom they had heard so much.

When they came to look their captors fairly in the face, to their great astonishment they recognized them as their rebel associates, with whom they had long been " hail, fellows, well met!"

The report turned out, in the end, to be a false alarm, — no Federal troops having at all left St. Joseph on such an expedition.

CHAPTER XIV.

"When the hurly-burly's done,
When the battle's lost and won."

HILE the rebels of Platte City and Platte County were in constant fear and expectation of being visited by Federal troops, they conducted themselves much better than they had done previously.   They, for a time, ceased mobbing, murdering, and persecuting Union men.   But, after so many false alarms about the coming of Federal soldiers, they began to think they wouldn't come at all, and directly commenced their work of violence again.

Near a week after the stampede, described in the preceding chapter, several hundred armed traitors were in Platte City, drilling and mustering. Late in the afternoon a runner came in, stating that a thousand Union soldiers were marching upon Platte City, and were already within a few miles of the place.

"The rascal wants to get up another stampede," said one of the rebel officers; "these fellows that are always coming in from the country to alarm us are abolitionists and deserve to be gibbeted."

"Hang him! hang him!" cried the rabble. And the excitement finally grew so high against the poor fellow that they actually seized him, put a rope round his neck, and were really upon the point of hanging him, when the Federal pickets made their appearance. In less than ten minutes the village was entirely deserted, except by some of the more intelligent slaves. Union citizens, for fear of being accused of turning informants, left also.

The Federals took possession of the deserted village, and lodged in the forsaken habitations of the fugitives.

The disloyal inhabitants supposed that the object of the expedition was to make arrests, and, consequently, made sure they would send out soldiers in every direction to hunt them up.

The weather being warm, and a full, round moon in the sky, no very great inconvenience could be anticipated from lying out.

A large number of the fugitives made for a wild, hilly region, a few miles north of Platte City. In the midst of these hills and ravines lived a very kind family in a neat little cottage perched on an eminence. This habitation was made the first rallying point for the portion of villagers who took their flight northward. The little domicile, however, was insufficient to accommodate one-tenth of the fugitives that collected around it.

There was but one Union man among them, and he, to his great astonishment, found himself marvellously popular all at once, after having been persecuted for months, mobbed at sundry times, and robbed of half his property, and that, too, by the same men who were now hanging on his skirts for protection.

The proprietor of the cottage finally proposed, as Mr. Rupert was a Union man, and likely to have the most influence with the Yankee soldiers, by whom they were momentarily expecting to be pursued, that he should stay at the cottage and take care of the ladies, while the men who were in danger of being arrested, should go and hide themselves.

This was agreed to; and the men, all except Rupert, made for a deep ravine not far from the house. About half-way down the steep declivity, on the hillside, grew a dense papaw thicket; in this dark place the cowardly rascals ensconced themselves.

By and by, one of their number, a young lawyer, who had great dread of the Yankees, began to feel some misgiving about the safety of their position; and, leaving his companions, he ascended the declivity to a point where a cornfield came to the brink, and, climbing over the fence, crouched in a corner among the weeds, where he was shaded from the light of the moon by tall green corn that grew near.

In the course of a few hours, the proprietor of the cottage, who was hid in the papaw thicket with the rest, concluded to reconnoitre in the direction of his dwelling, and ascertain, if possible, whether the Yankees had yet captured Rupert and his regiment of women.

In making his reconnoissance, he had necessarily to pass this fellow in the fence-corner. White, fleecy clouds were gliding like a procession of ghosts along the blue pavement of the skies, ever and anon obscuring the light of the moon. Taking advantage of these flying shadows, the reconnoitrer would glide along for a few paces, then pausing whenever the queen of night came out broad and bright. Under the feathery clouds, in a stooping posture, and with stealthy step, he moved along, holding his breath, and keeping a sharp lookout for the dreaded Yankees.

The cowardly lawyer, in the fence-corner, hearing a rustle in the leaves, lifted his head to look; and lo! within a few paces of him was the figure of a man, whose bent attitude and sly movement struck our knight of the bar as very suspicious. In a moment, the moon came out with her full, broad light, at which the reconnoitrer suddenly paused and squatted.

This movement instantly confirmed the terrible suspicions of the lawyer, that a bloody-minded Yankee sought his life, and was just then stooping to take aim.

With a yelp and a bound, the fellow left his hiding-place, and through the corn he dashed like a frightened buffalo, making the stalks and blades crack and rattle at a terrible rate.

The party in the papaw thicket, hearing the crashing in the cornfield, pricked up their ears in amazement. Some conjectured it was one thing and some another; but the most current suspicion seemed to be, that a cavalry charge was being made across the cornfield.

Meanwhile, the reconnoitrer, who had been the innocent cause of this new panic, stood dumfounded, not knowing whether he had raised a ghost, man, or demon.

The young lawyer ran, first in one direction, then in another; but finally made back for his friends in the papaw thicket. By this time the reconnoitrer had begun to retreat in the same direction; but, before he had advanced far down the declivity, the frightened fellow in the cornfield, coming full drive, reached the fence right opposite him, and, pausing not, in his terror, to consider ways or means, made a lunge! Over the fence he went with a tear, taking several rails along, which came down with a rattlety-bang! But on went the gallant knight, adown the frightful steep, first one end up, then the other, and, finally overtaking our retreating re-connoitrer, uptripped and forced him to join in a heels-over-head tumble to the neighborhood of the papaw thicket, — the party there con-cealed making sure, if the Devil hadn't broke loose, that at least a half-regiment of Yankees had. At all events, they deemed it inexpedient to await the result, or stop to ask any imperti-nent questions, but, taking to their heels, crossed the ravine in a trice, and through the forest they ran like a gang of wild horses.

Rupert and the women, hearing the noise and confusion, had sought a position where they had a fair chance of witnessing the whole perform-ance. An Irish girl in the group cried out, "St. Pater! what ligs they've goot!"

Believing themselves pursued, they continued their stampede several miles.

Scenes no less farcical were transpiring at the same time in a valley south of the village, whither, also, many of the citizens had fled. Most of the valley was covered thickly with large trees, the foliage of which almost entirely shut out the light of the moon. Here the frightened rebels hid themselves, some in one place, and some in another; and, all night long, individuals and groups were passing from place to place, and frequently frightening one another, producing panics and causing stampedes, by being mistaken for Union soldiers. A group nearest the village, early in the night, took fright at a herd of cattle and immediately took to their heels, running in the direction where most of the fugitives were concealed; at every jump skulking rebels started up, who mistook them for Yankees; and these, in their turn, while running for dear life, would, at every bound, start up others, who, in their turn, would run and frighten yet others, until a general stampede ensued.

The most laughable scene, during the night, took place between Dr. Muggins and Capt. Cock-

robin.   Each was groping through the dark valley hunting his wife, from whom he had been
separated in the last stampede.   They chanced
to meet; and each, taking the other for a
Yankee, bounded off to get behind a tree.

"There's one of them," said Muggins to himself, "peeping from behind a sturdy oak."

"Thunder and Mars!" exclaimed Cockrobin,
looking cautiously from behind a black walnut;
"that infernal Yankee's bent on shooting me,
else he wouldn't have taken a tree."

"Plague take the Federal!" added Muggins,
mentally; "he's trying to get a crack at me."

And there they stooped, peeped, and dodged,
each expecting from the other a bullet every
moment.

"I guess I'd better surrender," said Cockrobin
to himself; "I'd better be taken prisoner than
be shot here in the dark like a wolf."

"My Lord!" exclaimed Muggins to himself,
"it's terrible to think of being murdered right
here in the wild woods!   I'd better give myself
up to the confounded Yankee."

"Pray, don't shoot, stranger," cried Cockrobin; "I'll surrender."

"Zounds! just what I was going to propose to him," said the other to himself. "Then lay down your arms," demanded Muggins.

"I've got none," answered Cockrobin.

"Neither have I," confessed the other. "Who are you?"

"They call me Captain Cockrobin."

"Ha, ha! is that you, Cock? My name's Muggins."

"Good gracious, Dr. Mug. I took you for a tarnal Yankee. Have you seen anything of my wife?"

"No. Have you seen anything of mine?"

"Not a thing; nor wouldn't know her from a nigger if I should, in such a dungeon as this."

Just at this moment, a bevy of female rebels, having taken fright at a scared calf, came running toward them as fast as crinoline and balmoral would permit.

"Heaven save us!" cried Cockrobin, "the cavalry's coming!" and, wheeling about, they trusted to their heels to carry them out of harm's way.

The Union troops all this time, instead of being out scouting, were reposing on downy pillows in the village. And the next morning, at an early hour, they were on the march for Lexington.

CHAPTER XV.

" All are not men that wear the human form."

———

THE commotions of the country occasioned among secessionists a novel mixture of the elements of society. Men who had never mingled before as equals suddenly felt remarkable affinities and wonderful sympathies. The swellhead and the groundling, the nabob and the ragamuffin, to their mutual astonishment, all at once found themselves brethren and hail fellows, well met!

This was strikingly exemplified on the Fourth of July, at one of the saloons in Platte City. Surrounding a circular table, laden with cups and bottles, sat, cheek-by-jowl, Scallawag and Skedaddle, Dr. Puff and Patrick the scullion!

"By jabers," said Pat, "ond it's mysilf that don't want the nagers free—niver a bit! Now, Master

Skadaddle, af yer nagers roon away, jist coom for Patrick, the Irishmon, ond it's mysilf thot'll kotch em for ye, chaip as onybody;" saying which, he familiarly slapped Skedaddle on the back, and with as much emphasis as if he was killing rats.

"Remarkable!" exclaimed the nabob, springing up and down on his seat with great nervous agitation.

"What can detain Knickerbocker?" said Scallawag; "he was to have taken a bumper with us to-day, and so was Captain Si Gorden."

"No matter; let us drink!" responded Dr. Puff, at the same time taking up one of the bottles, and filling Skedaddle's goblet.

"Just so!" said the latter; "let us drink!" and, waiting not for the filling of the other cups, greedily emptied his own.

"Oh, ho! in good time!" exclaimed Knickerbocker, just coming in.

"After a long delay," said Scallawag. "Come, sit you down, my fine fellow, and try the flavor of our beverage."

"That I will," answered Knickerbocker, taking

a seat in the tippling-circle. "What have you, my chums? anything to make a poor devil forget his sins?"

"A sprinkle of the sparkling catawba and mellow champagne. I dare say, a good heavy potation will give you an easy conscience and a limber tongue, if not weak knees and a limber neck."

" You fill to the brim."

" Why not? — 'tis our heyday!"

" Then let us be jolly while we may."

" Just so! while we may!" said Skedaddle, turning off his second glass.

" Right!" remarked Dr. Puff; "for a man can't live always."

" Not even a secessionist," added Knickerbocker.

" Men of our political creed ought never to die," rejoined Puff.

" Indeed, that's so," said Knickerbocker; "for the Lord only knows where they'll go !"

Scallawag, who had taken it upon himself to be the master of ceremonies, — though innocent of any intention to pay for the wine, — having by this time filled the cups all round, said, "Now we lift our glasses and drink good health to all the pretty lasses."

"And grief to all Union lads and Black Republicans," added Dr. Puff.

"So mote it be!" said Scallawag.

"Just so! mote it be!" echoed Skedaddle, who, by this time, was getting pretty well elated.   And now jingling their glasses together, one against another, in token of good fellowship, they all drank at once, and with as much precision as a platoon could have let off a volley at the word *Fire!*

"You're a lucky dog, Knickerbocker," observed Scallawag, good-humoredly.

"So it would seem ; else old Ringtail would have got me long ago for keeping bad company."

"By jabers!" said Pat, half-aside ; "I count thot no dacent observation."

"The old man's death brought you a precious windfall, I understand. Heaven send I might be so fortunate ; but certain I never will."

"Poor devil! have you no father to die ? "

"Not one whose exit to kingdom-come is likely to turn out for me a windfall."

"Then let it be called a fall of wind."

"Upon my sowl," soliloquized Pat, "thase waked heritics jist aboot dith as af the fear o' the Divel was niver before their eyes."

"I thought your famous guerrilla chief, Si Gorden, was to have been with us on this occasion," remarked Knickerbocker.

"So he is," replied Dr. Puff; "at least, we expect him."

"Then I may yet hope to make his acquaintance."

"Come, let us prime our pans, prick our flints, and fire again," said Scallawag, at the same time filling the glasses.

"Wine, like woman's ruby lips, woos to kiss and come again," said Knickerbocker, as they all drank again.

"Ah, here comes the chief now!" exclaimed Dr. Puff, rising to his feet to greet the distinguished banditti leader.

"Your most obedient!" said the chief, coming forward loaded down with savage-looking weapons. A huge sword, awkwardly buckled to his girdle, hung dangling between his legs, and occasionally tripping him as he walked. His feet were ornamented with an enormous pair of shanghai spurs, to which were attached chains that clanked most barbarously as he walked.

After receiving an introduction to Knickerbocker, and making a very condescending bow, the chieftain seated himself; and, without waiting for ceremonies, seized the nearest bottle, filled a glass, and drank it down in a trice.

A Scotchman by the name of Crookshanks, who had been, but a few days before, robbed of a fine horse by this same guerrilla chief, chanced to see the scoundrel enter the saloon, and, eager to embrace the first opportunity of calling him to an account, followed him in.

By the time the chief was fairly in his chair, Crookshanks had planted himself just behind him, with his hand on the hilt of a short Scotch broadsword.

" You have a brave band, I understand, Captain Gorden," remarked Knickerbocker.

"You are right, sir," replied the captain; "my men are not afraid to face the Devil!"

"You intend joining General Price's army, I imagine?"

"Not I, by Jupiter! No, sir, no! Mine is an independent company; I've sot out on my own bottom."

"Oh, yes!" thundered the Scotchman at his back; "you've set out on your own bottom, but on my horse."

The astonished chief sprang to his feet; but in an instant Crookshanks had him by the throat.

"Villain! robber! cut-throat! fiend!" said the enraged Scotchman, "where's my horse?"

"Spare me! spare me!" cried the surprised and terrified wretch, most piteously.

"Remarkable!" exclaimed Skedaddle.

"Murther! murther!" cried Pat.

"You infernal marauder! thief! assassin!" continued the Scotchman, "where's my horse? Where's Widow Bedott's mules? Where's Miss Juniper's gold watch and diamond breastpin? Tell me, you robber."

"Spare, spare, oh, spare!" still cried the guilty wretch, gazing wildly at the gleaming blade that waved in fiery circles above his head.

"Call for the police!" bawled Dr. Puff.

"Just so,—for the police!" echoed Skedaddle.

"Bravo! it's good as a show!" said Knicker-bocker, who evidently enjoyed the scene im-measurably.

"My horse—I demand my horse," still thun-dered Crookshanks.

"I—I—I'll give him up, sir! I—I—I'll give him up!" stuttered the confused and frightened chief, backing, meanwhile, toward the door, and struggling to break from the strong grasp of his assailant, who held him as with a lion's paw.

In the midst of the confusion, Patrick slipped up to the table, and, turning his back on the company, emptied one of the bottles, then, wiping his mouth, cried, "Murther! murther!"

"Satisfied he had not been observed, and still feeling thirsty, as an Irishman will, he went slyly back to the table and emptied the other bottle. Then, wiping his mouth, as before, cried, —"Murther! murther!"

"Just so, — murder!" echoed Skedaddle.

Persistently Crookshanks held on to the robber's throat, and still waved the threatening blade above the cowering villain's head.

Dr. Puff kept saying, "Call for the police!"

While Scallawag, petrified with fear, did nothing but wildly stare.

Skedaddle, getting a little over his first excitement, happened to think that it would be a good time, amid the noise and confusion, to take a little more wine; so back he slyly glided to the table, and, taking up a bottle, peeped round to make sure that no one observed him, then, clapping it to his mouth, turned it up, up, up, till it reached the perpendicular; forced to believe it empty, he set it down, saying,—"Just so!" But, fully determined not to be altogether baffled, he now seized the other bottle, and, putting it to his mouth, turned it up, up, up, till it also reached the perpendicular; setting it down with unmoistened lips, an expression of wonder, and a look of melancholy disappointment, he said, "Remarkable!"

By this time, Crookshanks and the guerrilla

chief were in the street, and still struggling. The drawn blade, yet bloodless, glittered in the sunlight. The strong hand that bore it aloft was unaccustomed to deeds of violence; and to this alone the wretch, who deserved a thousand deaths, now owed his life.

Rebel policemen at length interfered, and the guerrilla chief was protected.

It may look almost too much to be believed, that this brigand should have been tolerated in Platte City, and allowed to go at liberty, when it was known to everybody that he was a robber and murderer. But a few days before the occurrence related above, he was guilty of one of the most barbarous deeds in the catalogue of crimes. Two young men belonging to a Union regiment, then at St. Joseph, having wandered out unarmed, on Sabbath day, a mile or two from the town, were captured by a scouting party of rebels, and taken to Platte City. This guerrilla chief, Si Gorden, hearing of the arrival of the prisoners, came dashing in with thirty armed men at his back, and demanded the young men. The writer of these pages, being present, protested against the prisoners' being put into the hands of the guerrillas; but what could one man do in opposing thirty? And what is argument, what reason and kind entreaty, to men who have neither hearts to feel nor brains to think?

The prisoners were taken just a little way out of the village, tied to a tree, and made targets of by these white-skinned savages. One of the young men, a youth scarce seventeen, upon his knees asked for time but to write a line to his widowed mother. He was answered with curses, and low, vulgar jests, more wicked than curses; and, while yet making the request, was mangled with bullets.

Incredible as it may appear, these murderers, the very next day, were given a sumptuous dinner by certain citizens of Platte City.

Note.—The author is willing to be sworn to the truth of the above statement. He has in no wise colored or exaggerated the facts. Si Gorden has since been shot.

CHAPTER XVI.

E here resume the story of the erring and unhappy Macqueen. The assassination he witnessed, as related in the twelfth chapter of this work, quite unbalanced his mind for a time; his insanity, however, was, fortunately, but temporary. On the same night of the assassination, after the shocking occurrence, he visited the Castle-room, where the Knights of the Golden Circle were in session; and, being wild with excitement, owing to the bloody scene he had just gazed upon, he furiously denounced the Order, calling them conspirators, murderers, demons, and everything that was vile and execrable. This bold and unlooked-for attack exasperated no less than it astounded the secret conclave of heartless assassins. They seized the offender at once, and, putting a gag in his mouth, cast him into a dungeon connected with the same building, which they called "The Place of Outer Darkness," and there kept him, unable to speak, and shut out from every ray of light, till their next meeting, which was the following night.

Knickerbocker, having obtained the password and some of the secret signs of the Order from an intoxicated Knight, whom he made believe that, during a recent visit to a neighboring town, he had joined the fraternity, was able to work himself into the Castle at Platte City without taking any oath or obligation. He was, therefore, present when Macqueen was gagged and cast into the dungeon. And, although he abhorred the barbarity of the treatment, dared not oppose the measure, for fear of being doomed himself to a similar fate. Nor did he dare, the next day, to lisp the affair into the public ear, knowing as he did that there were not enough of honest, law-abiding men in the whole county either to protect him or to rescue Macqueen from any punishment which the fiendish clan might be disposed to inflict upon him.

Mrs. Macqueen, supposing her husband was off on some sudden emergency to aid the wicked rebellion and plot treason, had made up her mind to discard him forever.

The following night, the members of the Order, Knickerbocker among the rest, met to determine the fate of the offender.

It was argued on the occasion that, if Macqueen was set at liberty, he would certainly do great injury to the Order, as well as harm to the cause of secession; and that to keep him imprisoned was equally unsafe. This view of the subject seemed to commend itself to the members generally. Knickerbocker, however, ventured to lift up his voice against it; but his effort to turn the scale and urge considerations of clemency was utterly unavailing; by an overwhelming vote, the unfortunate man was sentenced to die. He was then brought out of the dungeon, after having the gag removed from his mouth, and, in the presence of the whole circle, informed that he had but ten minutes to live, and that he could choose, if he wished, the manner of his death.

The delirium that had seized his brain the previous day was now gone; and he seemed in his right mind, but greatly exhausted, pale, and dejected.

"Only permit me to see my wife and children," said he, "and I will ask no more."

"Your request we cannot grant," responded the Chief of the Castle; "for the reason that such a permission would be unsafe for us, and might be highly prejudicial to the cause we seek to promote."

"I must see my wife and children," insisted the doomed man; "when that is over, I shall have lived long enough. I pledge my honor to return. Nor will I tell any one that I am to die by a decree of the Castle."

"We cannot risk you out of our hands," rejoined the Chief.

"He is a man of honor," said Knickerbocker;

17*

"I am not afraid to trust him, and will freely pledge my own life for his return. Allow him one hour to go and take leave of his wife and children; if he does not return, I will die in his stead. But I know he will redeem his promise, especially when to do otherwise would forfeit the life of a friend who takes such a risk in his behalf."

" Sooner would I die a thousand deaths than betray such a friend," said Macqueen; "I ask but one hour; let me go and embrace for the last time those who are far dearer to me than life, and invoke Heaven's blessing upon them. Confide in me, my friend; you shall not die in my stead."

"I do not fear it," replied Knickerbocker; "I beg that his request be granted. Humanity cannot do less."

The proposition was finally agreed to ; Knickerbocker was placed under guard, and Macqueen given liberty to visit his family.

The hour was late ; Mrs. Macqueen, after putting her little children to sleep, had thrown herself upon her couch, weary and wretched, to woo, if possible, " Nature's sweet restorer, balmy sleep." After a short and painful slumber, she started suddenly from her pillow, and began uneasily to walk the chamber-floor, saying, —

" From terrible *dreams* I wake to more terrible and distracting *thoughts*. Every joy is withered ; every prospect faded. All that's fair and bright upon the earth doth lose its beauty and sweetness." Now suddenly pausing, and ceasing a moment to breathe, she listened, — " Hark ! 'tis his footstep ; can it be he ? I shall lose my breath ; I must not speak to him. A traitor to his country, and the associate of black-hearted conspirators, I must learn to despise him."

With a look of unutterable anguish Macqueen entered the chamber. His wife turned scornfully from him.

" Florence" — said he, in a most touching and deeply-melancholy tone ; his voice faltered, and he could proceed no further.

" Leave me ! " said she, with a choked utterance and difficult breath, — " leave me, that I may utter no reproaches, — leave me, that you may be left alone to the judgments of Heaven and the accusations of your own conscience."

"I will, I will!" replied he, with heart-breaking emotion.

"Then go at once that my blood may not congeal in my veins."

"Ah, I perceive that my presence is a pestilence to you."

"An incubus, rather, producing that strange sensation we call the nightmare."

"It was not always so, Florence."

"Pray let me forget that it ever was otherwise."

"Would to Heaven we could each grow oblivious of happier days, or else blot from recollection that which has marred their joys and dimmed their brightness forever. I am about to leave you, Florence, and forever. I have come to take a final leave of you and our dear children."

"What mean you?"

"Question me not; my time is short."

"You are mad, and surely know not what you say."

"Too well I know my fate, which is a sad one. I deserve to die; yet fain would I live to win back the lost love you once cherished for me, and to prove to you that, amid scenes of trial and misfortune, I have grown wiser and better."

"My husband, why do you look and talk so strange?"

"Let me see my dear children. This night I am to die; ask me not by whose hands. My honor is pledged; I must speedily return."

"You shall not go, my husband! you shall not go!" cried the frantic wife, seizing hold of him.

"I pray you, detain me not; a friend has pledged his life for my return; should I fail, he must die in my stead. I know you would not have me prove so treacherous."

"O Heaven! what can this mean?" cried the frantic woman, so bewildered in mind she scarcely knew whether it was a dream or a reality.

"Heaven give you fortitude, Florence. And now I crave that you may forget my follies and forgive my errors.   And, above all, I pray you, teach our children to fear God, love their country, and practise virtue.   Now let me see and embrace my sleeping babes."

"Merciful Heaven! I cannot endure this," exclaimed the distracted woman, wringing her hands in heart-broken anguish.

At this juncture, Knickerbocker abruptly entered the apartment.

"My God!" exclaimed Macqueen, in overwhelming surprise; "what means this, Knickerbocker?   How does it happen you are here?"

"As Heaven would have it, a detachment of Federal cavalry just now came dashing into town.   Our infernal conclave being seized with a panic, every man was left to take care of himself, and I among the rest.   God be praised! we shall both live to see these accursed traitors hung."

The effect of the tidings upon Mrs. Macqueen can be better imagined than described.

The Federal soldiers, that night and during the next day, made thirty-nine arrests, a majority of whom were Knights of the Golden Circle. The prisoners were taken to St. Joseph, persuaded to take the oath of allegiance, and then turned loose, murderers and all.

As soon as these wretches got home, they were tenfold worse, if possible, than before; robbery, house-burning, and murder were carried on with an unsparing hand.

The extreme clemency of our Federal officers was a great mistake. The reckless rebels construed it into cowardice; and, invariably, the more kindly they were treated, the more ungrateful, daring, and treacherous they became.

Macqueen and family, Knickerbocker, Parson Southdown and lady, with several other Union families, left Platte City in company with the Federal soldiers, and went, some into Iowa, some to Illinois, and others to Indiana.

No sooner had the released rebel prisoners got home from St. Joseph than they burnt the houses of Macqueen, Southdown, and other loyal citizens who had left the country to save their lives.

CHAPTER XVII.

" Our eagle shall rise 'mid the whirlwinds of war,
And spread his wide wings o'er the tempest afar."

THE reader will hardly need to be reminded where we left our youthful hero, Adrian Malvin. Though on freedom's soil, and out of the reach of his enemies, who thirsted for his blood, he was not long content to remain an idle spectator of events at such an eventful period. Beginning to comprehend more fully the nature of the strife, and to see that it was a deadly struggle between civilization and barbarism, freedom and slavery, republicanism and aristocracy, loyalty and treason, his anxiety to take part in the conflict became intense. And scarcely less patriotic than himself was Simon, the fugitive slave whom he had assisted to rescue his wife and children from bondage. Especially was Simon fired with an ambition to have a hand in striking a telling blow for freedom in behalf of his own down-trodden race. He had frequent interviews with Malvin on the subject, who deeply sympathized with him in his noble and philanthropic aspirations. All the while they were but biding their time; each kept steadily before his mind the great purpose, and anxiously awaited an opportunity to play their part in the fearful tragedy.

Simon had two brothers and a sister still in slavery; and now, having tasted the sweets of freedom himself, and learned to appreciate the boon, he began to meditate the daring project of rescuing them also from the hell of slavery.

He laid his scheme before Malvin, who, after due deliberation, approved, and agreed to aid him in it. They immediately went to work, and made up a company of seventy-nine colored men, most of whom had been slaves.

About this time, Gen. James Lane, with a considerable force of Kansas men, was preparing to make a dash into southwestern Missouri, to avenge outrages upon Union citizens there, who had suffered more than tongue can tell, and to chastise certain guerrilla bands, whose barbarity had been incredible and revolting.

Malvin, who was the chosen leader of the seventy-nine colored men, deemed it expedient to move at the same time Gen. Lane did, and to keep in reach of his army so long as he went in the right direction. There was wisdom in this policy; for Lane's name was a terror to all the rebels of Missouri; everywhere he went they fled before him. To follow in his wake, therefore, was to secure protection against overwhelming numbers.

Lane's march was rapid. Malvin kept within a few miles of him till they got as far into southwestern Missouri as Lane chose to penetrate, which was within a day's march of the Arkansas line.

Malvin's expedition may look rather rash, if not altogether reckless; but we must bear in mind that he had good reason to suppose the fighting rebels on his route would be chiefly occupied in rallying at some given point to meet Lane, and, consequently, that no very strong force could be collected to oppose him in his rapid march through the country. After getting fairly out from under Lane's protecting wing, he sent Simon a mile or more in advance of the main body of his little army, with the instruction, whenever he came in sight of anybody, to dash forward as if flying for his life, and at the top of his voice shout, "Jim Lane! Jim Lane!"

This worked like a charm; the name of Jim Lane was more terrifying than "an army with banners." The inhabitants of the country everywhere fled in dismay. Malvin's seventy-nine men, in the eyes of frightened and guilty rebels, looked at least a force ten thousand strong, especially while the name of *Jim Lane* was ringing in their ears.

Near the Arkansas line, at an abrupt turn of the road, and descending a deep declivity into a narrow valley, Simon came suddenly upon a camp of Texan rangers, accompanied by several hundred Indians. At once he raised his voice to its highest pitch, and cried, "Jim

Lane! Jim Lane! Ten thousand men! ten thousand men! Right upon you! right upon you!"

He halted, pointing with outstretched arm and ominous look in the direction he had come. A deathlike stillness for a moment reigned throughout the encampment; and, while the astonished warriors yet held their breath, lo! the heavy tread of many horses' feet was heard over the hills and jutting cliff.

"Hark! they come! they come!" cried Simon. "Fly! fly for your lives, my countrymen!"

That was sufficient; the panic was complete; and the stampede was like the sudden rush of noisy waters when a milldam breaks, or a swollen river overleaps its banks. Down the valley they went, red savages and white savages, leaving everything behind,—guns, ammunition, horses, provisions, and all their equipage.

Malvin and his men, hearing the racket, rode hastily to the bluff, and had the satisfaction of witnessing the stampede.

Taking possession of the horses which the enemy had left behind, and whatever else they could make serviceable and were able to carry with them, they hastened on, still using the formidable name of Jim Lane wherever it was deemed necessary. And thus they were able to proceed, without fighting a battle and without opposition, to Scallawagville, which they reached in the night-time, just before day,— and captured without firing a gun.

In the vicinity of the place, and before reaching the town, they came upon a guerrilla camp, and surprised and captured the whole band. Among them was Tom Bolton, the former master of Simon's wife. This was particularly gratifying to Simon, who knew the villain well, and had a vivid recollection of his inhumanity to slaves.

Malvin also knew most of the guerrillas, as many of them were in the mob that so maltreated him and Parson Elmore.

Seven of the band were accused by some respectable citizens in the community of murdering Union men in the neighborhood, and also of having killed, in the most cruel manner, several free negroes, without any provocation.

18*

After a fair trial, the seven were convicted, upon undoubted testimony, not only of wilful murder, but of torturing some of their victims in the most savage and brutal manner. Within a few hours after their conviction and sentence, they were hung. Among the number was Tom Bolton.

The men who gave testimony against the assassins well knew that their own lives were insecure if they remained in the country after the departure of Malvin and his soldiers; so they made up their minds at once to go with them to Kansas.

Upon taking possession of the place, Malvin, of course, proclaimed martial law, and threw out pickets in every direction, both to guard against being surprised, and to prevent the inhabitants of the village from leaving.

The first day was mainly consumed trying and executing the guerrillas. In the morning of the following day, Malvin learned that a considerable rebel force was being collected a short distance from the village for the purpose of attacking him; and, fearing his retreat would be cut off, he began to make hasty preparations for a departure. He had already proclaimed to the slaves, in the town and vicinity, that all who wished for freedom might find protection under the stars and stripes if they would consent to go with him to Kansas. This proclamation at once added upwards of fifty able-bodied men to his force; and, being abundantly supplied with horses, arms, and ammunition, which they had taken from the Texan rangers and Indians, he was prepared, not only to equip and mount these recruits, but also to furnish horses, wagons, and provision, for near a hundred slave women and children, who were also begging to be taken to the land of freedom.

Simon was now thrown into great perplexity about his sister, who was three miles out of the village, and in the vicinity where the rebels were concentrating. He had found and armed his two brothers; but his anxiety to rescue his sister from the miseries and degradation of slavery was intense; and the only and last opportunity was now passing. The time set to leave the place was within one hour of expiring.

He had learned where his sister was, but the chances seemed ten to one against him in any attempt to get her away; yet he could not make up his mind to leave without making the trial, though it was certain it would be at the peril of his life. Mounting his horse, he dashed away at full speed; a few minutes brought him in sight of her master's residence. He discovered several armed men standing at the gateway, and felt sure that one of two things would certainly happen, — that he would either frighten those men into a precipitate flight, or else become their prisoner if not a dead man at their feet. Putting spurs to his horse, he dashed on at full speed, and as soon as he was in hearing, rose in his stirrups, and at the top of his voice cried, "They're coming! they're coming!"

"Heavens and earth! we're goners!" exclaimed Remington, the master of the slave-girl that Simon was after; "nothing but our legs can save us." And off he went as if old Splitfoot had been at his heels; and after him followed the rest, on the double-quick.

As Simon drew near, Rachel, his sister, recognized and ran out to meet him. He dismounted and clasped her in his arms.

"Now is your time, sister," said he, "to go to the land of freedom."

"Praise the good Lord!" exclaimed Rachel, with difficult utterance, so overcome was she with emotion. "Let us hurry, then," added she; "they'll be after us."

"Whose horse and buggy is this?" inquired Simon, at the same time seizing the rein of an elegant gelding that stood ready harnessed to a fine, new vehicle.

"It is master's," replied Rachel.

"Jump in, quick!" said Simon. And in a trice the two were in the carriage and going like the wind!

Remington and his companions, having paused to look back when they reached the hemp-field fence, saw Simon embrace Rachel. This awakened their suspicions that the alarm-cry was but a ruse; and when they looked and listened in vain for the enemy, this suspicion was greatly strengthened. By the time Simon and his sister were fairly seated in the buggy, Remington and his armed companions were making the best time they could toward the contrabands, swearing like pirates, and with loud yells commanding them to stop.

"Hold on there!—hold on there!" shrieked Remington, as if catching his last breath; at the same time making his long legs go like winding blades, or rather like the ungainly wings of a windmill in a stiff breeze.

"Halt! or be shot!" cried a savage-looking rascal, pointing his gun at the fugitives. They might as well have talked to the winds or raved at the clouds. On went the sable hero and heroine, for they were in high glee, drove an excellent horse, and rode in a splendid carriage.

Remington's eyes being riveted upon his fast-receding horse, buggy, and slave, he left his flying feet and winding legs to take care of themselves; but, having no organs of vision, they came very abruptly in collision with an awkward stump, that evidently had very little respect for Southern chivalry, and certainly no heart to feel for a distressed man who had just lost a slave. This collision which happened to the lower extremities, suddenly brought about a collision of the upper extremity with old mother earth. It was funny to see the fellow on his head, while his legs, up in the air, seemed to imagine they were still running, and kept on in vigorous motion.

"Shoot! shoot!" he shouted to his companions, before he had fairly recovered his feet. Immediately, several guns were fired at the fugitives, who, by that time, were quite out of harm's way. The discharge of the guns only served to frighten Simon's saddle-horse, which he had left standing in the road. The animal, seeming to take the hint that he was among enemies, now scampered away after his master, and followed him into town. Simon and Rachel just got in in good time to march out with the company. As they came up, full drive, in front of the ranks of mounted men, the soldiers doffed their caps, and, swinging them round and round, sent up a shout that made the welkin ring.

Having taken possession of all the arms and ammunition they could find in town, Malvin felt confident that the rebels of the place could not equip themselves in time to follow and give him battle ; yet he entertained some apprehensions from another quarter.

Their march was rapid, and continued till after midnight. Coming to a good watering-place, they halted, took refreshment, rested till morning light, and, by the time the orb of day flung his mantling splendors o'er the dewy hills, the cavalcade was in motion.

About noon that day, Malvin learned that he was pursued by a rebel force of three or four hundred mounted men. This news quickened their steps. Malvin, knowing that his new recruits were entirely undisciplined and knew almost nothing about the use of fire-arms, determined to avoid a battle if possible.

By the time he reached Missouri, he found that the enemy was close upon his heels. Placing the women and children in front and his best disciplined men in the rear, he ordered a rapid movement. Knowing that General Lane was still in southwestern Missouri, and inferring that the inhabitants of the country were in a state of great confusion, he had but little fear of being attacked in front; all his attention, therefore, was directed to the enemy that hung upon his rear.

At length, discovering that the foe was fast gaining upon him, he began to look out for a suitable spot to make a stand and give battle to his pursuers. Pretty soon, they approached a hill, or rather a succession of hills, rising one above another,—something like terraced grounds, or embankments, ascending in regular gradations; after reaching the summit, Malvin ordered a halt, selected a few men to accompany the women and children, who were to continue their march as long as they were able to hold out before encamping, and then commanded his soldiers to form a line of battle.

By this time, the enemy was in full view in the valley below, and presented a formidable appearance compared to Malvin's little army.

Near the chosen battle-ground, a round-topped mound reared its lofty head, overlooking all the region in the direction of the enemy. Malvin ordered the fairest-complexioned of his men to form a procession and march round and round that mound, that the enemy might be led to think they were being reinforced. In order that the deception might be more certain and complete, they hastily prepared a variety of banners, that every time they came round in sight of the enemy they might display a different-shaped or different-sized flag.

The procession soon commenced, and, as they came round in sight of the enemy, the black negroes, who remained in line of battle, raised a tremendous shout, as they were directed to do, to give the impression that they were exulting over the arrival of reinforcements. Round and round the procession went, first carrying one banner and then another; and sometimes on horseback, appearing to be cavalry, and sometimes on foot, representing infantry.

While this was going on, a battery was erected on top of the mound, and mounted with black logs resembling cannon.

No sooner had these counterfeit cannon made their appearance than the rebels in the valley began to turn their faces toward Arkansas. In a very short space of time they entirely disappeared. No doubt their imaginations smelt General Jim Lane in the wind.

Well pleased with the success of this stratagem, Malvin again moved on. At two other points only, in his progress through the country to Kansas, was he threatened with an attack, and at each of these, the enemy was put to flight by Simon's trick of riding ahead in a gallop, and crying, "Jim Lane! Jim Lane."

Upon reaching the free soil of Kansas, these sable men and women, and brave adventurers, raised such a shout as never before was heard in the wilds of the West. Parson Elmore, who had been on a recruiting expedition in Iowa, had just returned, and was the first to greet and congratulate the brave men who had imperilled their lives for the good of their country and the freedom of the oppressed.

CHAPTER XVIII.

"And the brute crowd, whose envious zeal
Huzzas each turn of Fortune's wheel,
And loudest shouts when lowest lie
Exalted worth and station high."

PARSON Southdown, having fled from Missouri to southern Illinois, found directly that he had but got out of the frying-pan into the fire. In the vicinity where he temporarily stopped, the tories were making up a regiment to help the rebels. And their abuse and persecution of loyal men who enlisted under the stars and stripes, so far as vile tongues could go, exceeded anything the parson had met with among the Border-ruffians of Missouri. To be sure, the tories of Illinois did not murder Union men, as did the Missouri rebels, but, manifestly, it was only for the want of courage that they did not.

They openly justified the assassinations, rob-
beries, and house-burnings, committed by the
marauders and guerrilla bands of Missouri.

Parson Southdown, for proposing to address
the people on the state of the country, and to
give a narrative of what he had seen and ex-
perienced among the rebels, was threatened with
tar and feathers. Yet these same tories made
a loud profession of being peace men, and in
favor of free speech.

It was not until Mr. Douglas made his famous
loyal speech, at Springfield, Illinois, putting an
extinguisher on the treasonable project of sending regiments from Illinois to help the South
fight against the Union, that any man dared
make a loyal speech in that region of country.

Mr. Douglas's utterances had long been law
and gospel throughout southern Illinois, and,
as soon as it was known that he was for putting
down the rebellion, the party-leaders under him
said to the mustering tories, "Disband!" and
they disbanded. They said to the loud-mouthed,
brainless rabble, "Hold your tongues!" and
they suddenly became dumb dogs.

19*

Not that their principles were changed in the least; but they had been accustomed to follow their leaders, and fear no danger.

Parson Southdown at length ventured to publish that he would lecture, in the village where he was stopping, on the subject of the rebellion. The disloyal citizens were somewhat divided as to the propriety of allowing him to speak; after a good deal of contention, however, they concluded to let him address the people, provided he would go for the Union and the Constitution.

It is a noteworthy fact, that traitors and tories who think it expedient to disguise their disloyalty, at once begin to glorify the Union as it was, and the Constitution as it is. And when they want an excuse to rail against the government, they dwell upon the cruelty of the war and the immense loss of life and property attendant upon it. But they are careful to say nothing of the barbarity and fiendishness of the rebels. Let any one mention a great crime, or a shocking murder, committed by traitors or slave-driving demons, and the class of men just mentioned are ready in a moment to find an excuse for the inhumanity. If the Union troops burn a town, through military necessity, they are called vandals, thieves, incendiaries. But when it is said that a gang of rebels surprised a Union family at dead of night, and murdered the head of the house in the presence of his family, then robbed and burnt the dwelling, or when it is told, that a neighborhood or village has been surprised, pillaged, burnt, and the inhabitants indiscriminately massacred, these tories, straightway, begin to make excuses for them. "They were exasperated. The abolitionists have made them mad. Their niggers have been stolen or persuaded away, and that's vastly provoking." Thus they go on. Is it not plain whose side they are on?

The author of these pages has heard this class of men, even in New England, apologizing for the late terrible massacre at Lawrence, Kansas. "The fanatical abolitionists were the cause of it," say they. "The people of Missouri have been imposed upon by the Kansas Yankees; they can't expect anything better."

To hear such an outrage excused, to hear

such cowardly murderers apologized for, is enough to set any honest man's heart on fire, and send his hot blood tingling through every vein.

Only think of it! eight hundred armed ruffians and assassins, going stealthily, and in the dead of night, upon an unarmed, unwatched, and sleeping village, and with fire and sword spreading death and destruction in every direction; rushing into private houses, butchering husbands and brothers in the presence of wife, children, mother, sisters, — an inhumanity, a savage cruelty, too horrid to think about. Yet men there are in our midst, and not a few, who are fain to apologize for this barbarity. "These men have lost their niggers, and are provoked." Oh, specious excuse for indiscriminate butchery! "*Tory, traitor, copperhead*," are names too mild for such disloyal wretches, — quite too mild, no matter where they belong, or in what country they may live.

The evening at length came round for Parson Southdown's lecture. The hall was crowded with all sorts of people; and mixed in with the throng were scores of the most gallows-looking reprobates that ever escaped the gibbet.

"Now," muttered some of these unwashed, uncombed groundlings, "if he says anything in favor of the niggers, we'll howl him down, or else take him out and hang him."

It is remarkable how mean men detest the colored race. It is true, the world over, that the lower and more degraded a white man is, the worse he hates a black man.

The parson, without any apologies, thus began:—

"Men of Illinois! it is a dark hour for our country; there is treason at the South, and treachery in the North. You know something of what has happened in the Slave States: the people, in their madness, have pulled down upon their own heads the direst calamities. Alas, what bloodshed and desolation I have witnessed there! And what sorrows! what heart-breaking! And the end is not yet. Designing men are struggling for power; and dull-brained and malignant-hearted creatures —

hardly to be called men — are made their tools.
And these soulless, brutal miscreants. delighting
to do mischief, rush headlong and remorselessly into the fearful tragedy. We have seen
the ruin which tracks their progress.

"Believe me, the same elements exist in the
free North. You, here, are hanging upon the
brink of a volcano, — a volcano, swelling, seeth-
ing, quivering, for its upheaval! Should the
eruption come, woe to this land! All that is
now fair and beautiful will be quickly effaced
and speedily blotted out. And who will be to
blame but yourselves? It is for you to say
whether you will have peace and prosperity in
this bright land, or war and desolation.

"You have among you many reckless men
who are utter strangers to any feeling or sentiment of patriotism; and have never taken
thought about what it is to have a country, —
a free country, — who have no appreciation of a
government, and who know not how to prize
good and wholesome laws. This class of men
readily become the tools of unscrupulous politicians, demagogues, and partisans.

"If there is any difference between Southern traitors and Northern tories, that difference is in favor of the former; for they are greatly blinded by their hot blood and fiery passions, and by what they think their interests; while the disloyal men of the North are cool, calculating knaves, snakes in the grass, and very appropriately called "Copperheads."

At this, the *great unwashed* began to hiss.

"There they are now!" exclaimed the parson; "don't you hear them hiss? According to natural history, there are but two creatures that hiss, — the goose and the serpent. The latter hisses from malice, and the former for the want of sense. I shall leave it for the hissing bipeds of the present assembly to determine for themselves as to which class they belong.

"Conspiracies and conspirators are not all at the South; plotting villany is at work in the North; intrigue is busy and sedition rife!"

Now again the ruffians got up an interruption, — groaned and howled, and behaved in the most unseemly manner. But the parson, elevating his strong, trumpet-toned voice, went on:

"Secret conclaves, bent on direst mischief, and aiming at the overthrow of the government, infest almost every precinct in this country."

A politician in the audience, a vaporing demagogue, who stood at the head of a Castle, or fraternity of the Golden Circle, that held their secret meetings in the place, taking the parson's last sentence for a fling at their Order, poured forth a torrent of oaths, low slang, and disgraceful billingsgate, which, though highly offensive to ears polite, yet seemed exactly to the taste of that portion of the crowd which belonged to the *great unwashed*. They applauded the blackguard to the echo, while they cursed Parson Southdown for an abolition refugee, whom the slave-holders should have shot or hung.

Heeding little their furious threats and demonstrations, the speaker said,—

"Do you ask me what motive men can have at the North for turning traitors, acting a disloyal part, and trying to trammel the wheels of the government? I can readily tell you. Chiefly are they actuated by party rancor.

They would even punish themselves for the sake of gratifying their malice against a party, which, to their infinite mortification, has, in a fair race, gained a victory over them. Besides, the only hope the disloyal party can have of ever again coming into power is that of joining hands with the rebels. The traitors north of Mason and Dixon's line may profess to be Union men, but they mean, all the while, a union with the slave-holding power. The disappointed office-seekers of this country are the ringleaders in the disloyal movement which is making so much trouble. They are unscrupulous, time-serving men, who, for the sake of office, would unhesitatingly make an agreement with hell, and enter into compact with Satan himself." Here the rabble howled and hissed again.

"I tell you plainly," continued the parson, "from north to south, from east to west, the sworn enemies of freedom, the sworn enemies of law and order, of right, truth, justice, are marshalling their clans, and banding themselves together for the most diabolical purpose that ever actuated depraved men. Their determination is to *rule* or *ruin*. If they cannot control the government, they want to break it up. If they cannot hold the helm of the ship of state, they want to see it dashed upon the rocks.

"Think me no fanatic. I know these men, and I am acquainted with their brethren in Rebeldom. They are of the same spirit; they have the same howl, the same hiss, and the same growl; and they are aiming at the same end, — why should they not sympathize?

"This combination against the government, on the part of the traitors of the South and the tories of the North, should suggest to loyal men and patriots the necessity of joining hand to hand, and standing shoulder to shoulder, in the great conflict, which is now inevitable and already begun, and the result of which is destined to tell upon future ages, and to settle, it may be, certain important and vexed questions for all time to come.

"It shocks me, fellow-citizens, to hear so many of you talk as though it mattered little whether the government should stand or fall. Civilized and Christianized as we claim to be, if we should be left without a government, a very few years would suffice to see us lapsed into barbarism.

"It is a time for patriots to do their duty and stand by their suffering country. We are passing through a fearful crisis. Everything is imperilled,—liberty, religion, and all we hold sacred are imperilled. Can we be silent or inactive at such a time? Shall we sleep at our posts, or resign ourselves to indifference, while tyrants are upon the alert, while conspirators are stealing forth with foul intent, and while the political incendiary, torch in hand, enters the citadel which we, as patriots, are set to defend? Forbid it, Almighty God!

"The wise and good of all nations have ever reckoned *patriotism* among the highest and brightest of human virtues; and very justly; for, without this virtue, governments, whether good or bad, could have no stability, nor the best institutions of a country the least security. A patriot may, I grant, seek to improve or to reform the government under which he lives by an appeal to enlightened reason and to the principles of truth and justice. But he will not, for a light cause, desire revolution, much less to kindle the terrible fires of civil war. Rebellion can only be justified in cases of great oppression, injustice, and tyranny, on the part of a government; because rebellion and revolution seldom occur without fearful disaster and an immense cost of blood and treasure, and, if successful, generally result in rending, upheaving the foundations, and overturning the whole superstructure of a government, thereby destroying much, if not all, that's good and valuable connected with it, besides wrecking private fortunes and causing a vast destruction of public and private property, as well as loss of life, depraving of manners, and serious detriment to morality and religion. As long as evils are at all bearable, rebellion is scarcely justifiable, even in a *bad* government, owing to the dire calamities and untold suffering it never fails to bring with it. What, then, should be thought of the men who, from motives of ambition and self-aggrandizement, can enter into conspiracy against a *good* government, — treacherously attempt its overthrow, and recklessly precipitate their country into bloody revolution ?

"What should be thought of American citizens who, not content with the God-given heritage of peace and plenty, not content with our national greatness and prosperity, not content with our glorious Union, not content with the best government upon the face of the whole earth, and not satisfied with having been pampered, petted, and flattered by a too indulgent government, not satisfied with having been allowed to monopolize the fairest portion of our fair land, not satisfied with having grown rich by piracy and kidnapping, — ay, not satisfied with having enslaved millions of human beings, wringing from their weary hands, year after year, unpaid toil, and holding them in a state of the most abject and cruel bondage, — what, I repeat, should be thought of American citizens who, not content, not satisfied, with all these advantages, and being indulged in the practice of all these enormities, yet seek to ruin the government that has built them up, and

20*

that has honored, shielded, and protected them? Ay, and who, to compass that ruin, have been guilty of perjury, treachery, plunder, and murder! What, I ask, should be thought of such American citizens?

"The men who made this revolution, who inaugurated the disastrous civil war that is upon us, have long received unmerited honors at the hands of the government they are now trying to destroy; they have had lavished upon them far more than their share of Federal patronage and Federal offices. Instead of being grateful for undeserved favors, they, meanwhile, only grew the more insolent, arrogant, overbearing, and dictatorial. And, at last, because, forsooth, the slave-power was not allowed to continue dominant at Washington,—after having almost ruined the government,— these vile and unprincipled men, flying into a passion, began at once to set mischief on foot, and to lay plans for the rending and utter subversion of the Union. And it comes out that to *rule or ruin* has been their secret motto for years; and that, while pretending to serve the government, they were, even then, but a secret conclave of black-hearted traitors, plotting the disruption of the Union and the overthrow of the government.

"And only think of the means resorted to in order to make the revolution a success,—how diabolical! Equally abhorrent to religion and humanity, and calculated to kindle feelings of irrepressible indignation in every feeling heart.

"A mode of warfare has been sanctioned by the leaders in this war for the destruction of the Union that will stamp eternal disgrace upon Southern character, and justly excite the world's abhorrence!

" But cruelty, brutality, selfishness, and fiendishness, belong not exclusively to the South. Northern men, who take sides with such wretches, excuse their barbarity, give countenance to and manifest sympathy for them in their career of crime, are no better than they.

" Men of Illinois, those of you who are seeking to throw obstacles in the way of the administration, while struggling to roll back the dark and desolating wave of revolution, quell insurrection, crush the wicked rebellion, restore law and order, and give peace to the country, are traitors of the worst type, and deserve to hang by the neck!"

At this, the politician again began to swear, rant, and rave. The groundlings, who looked to him as their leader, immediately joined in, making a tremendous uproar.

Being well armed, and knowing how to use revolvers in cases of emergency, the parson had but little fear of bodily injury. Amid the confusion he still kept on : —

"To my certain knowledge, Northern tories, and especially disloyal editors, in this and other non-slave-holding States, have done and are still doing much to prolong the terrible, sanguinary strife in which we are engaged. Many young men of Missouri, now in the rebel army, were induced to enlist under the stars and bars, in opposition to the stars and stripes, by reading a class of disloyal Northern papers, with which Missouri is inundated. These incendiary and seditious sheets are full of lying invective and inflammatory denunciation against the administration, the national currency, and the Federal army. The war, which is purely one of self-defence on the part of the government, and waged but to preserve the existence and save the life of the nation, is called a Lincoln war, a Black-Republican war, an abolition war, &c. And they are continually telling the armed traitors, that great meetings are being held all over the Northern States for the purpose of putting a stop to the war. They tell the rebels of the South, that their country is invaded by vandal hordes from the North, who seek to trample upon their rights and reduce them to slavery. And, all the while, they ignore the fact that the slave-holders of the South began the war, and that the Federal government has only met this appeal to arms, by the arbitrament of the sword and the stern process of war, for the purpose of vindicating the supremacy of the laws and putting down a causeless rebellion.

"The effect of these disloyal newspapers is to induce the belief, in the minds of the rebels, that there is a large and growing party at the North in sympathy with them, and whose influence will soon be sufficient to paralyze the arm of the Federal government, and so cripple the power of the administration as to insure success to the revolution.

"And these reprobates are the more wicked in thus sowing the seeds of sedition and encouraging rebellion, because of their hypocrisy. They really have no wish for the ultimate success of the rebel arms and a division of the country; no! their hope is to have the war continue, while they seem to oppose it, till the next presidential election, in order to have a chance to reproach and displace the party in power. Then they expect to take the Southern traitors in their arms, saying, —

"'We have been your friends all the while; now, just come back into the Union and help us beat the Republicans, and we'll make slavery the chief corner-stone of the government.'"

.   .   .   .

As to a majority of his hearers, the parson was but "casting pearls before swine;" they had neither the honesty to receive the truth, nor minds to comprehend and feel the force of argument.

And right here lies the great danger, — dai

ger to our country and its free institutions, danger to the Republic,—the ignorance and viciousness of a very large class, both of foreigners and native-born Americans. To carry this uncultured, unreflecting herd, and make them their tools, designing men have only to appeal to their prejudices and inflame their passions. And when such appeals are made, these brutal men are ready either to *vote* or to *mob*, as the knaves who play upon their passions and prejudices may dictate.

The truth of this has been abundantly exemplified of late, at New York, Boston, Detroit, and in various localities throughout Indiana, Ohio, and Illinois.

In New York, fifty thousand of these degraded human beings were set on by the disloyal press of that city, and by certain copperhead politicians, to trample down law and order, burn public property, pillage, rob, and murder. And this barbarous conduct their apologists, who had cunningly instigated them to commit such brutal outrages, called resisting the draft. "These poor men don't want to go fight against their brethren at the South," say the copperheads. Yet these same "poor men" think no hardship of killing innocent people in the streets of New York,—and people, too, no more to blame for the draft than the inhabitants of another planet.' The negroes they murdered were just as liable to the draft as themselves. To kill these harmless black men was rather a strange way of resisting the draft.

The truth is, *plunder* was the main object; and the wire-workers behind the curtain hoped to have their political enemies robbed and murdered.

CHAPTER XIX.

"But endless is the list of human ills ;
And sighs might sooner cease than cause to sigh."

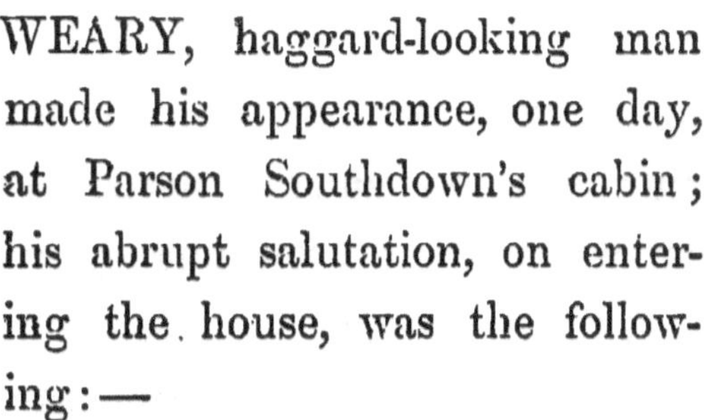

A WEARY, haggard-looking man made his appearance, one day, at Parson Southdown's cabin; his abrupt salutation, on entering the house, was the following:—

"I've hurn that you're a preacher from Missouri, an' a refugee; now I'm from Missouri, too; come from way down the lower eand of the State, whur it jines on to Arkansaw. I wur run off by them 'bom'nable grillers, case I kind o' stuck up for the ole Union. The blasted critters wanted to hang me, whether or no; so my nighest neighbor, Jim Cooly, found out what was gwien on, an' he steps in, an' jist in time. Oh dear! it riles me when I think about it. As I was gwien to say, one minute later, and I'd been strung up by the neck, with nothin' to stand on but the naked air; an' wouldn't that 'ave been a purty sight for my poar wife an' children? But what would them tarnal grillers have kured for that? —the savage heathens! But as I was sayin', Jim Cooly steps in, jist in the nick of time, an' pulls out a bottle of whiskey from his pocket, an' hands it to the rascal who wus jist gwien to tie the rope round my neck. You may depend on it, stranger, I felt mighty quare. Well, you see, the hangman, he kotch hold of the bottle; an' while he wus swollerin' the licker, an' the rest wur crowdin' up to take their turn, Cooly, he hunched me, an' whispered in my yur what I'll never forgit ef I live to be as old as Jerusalem. He said, says he, 'What's your legs made for?' Depend on it, I took the hint quicker nor lightning. Then says he, 'Cut stick, you fool! nor don't stop tell you git t'other side of the north pole.' Jehosophat! you orter seen me run across the turnip-patch. I fairly split the wind; an' wust of all, I didn't have time to say farewell to Sally an' the children. An' so, you see, I've kept gwien tell I've got hur; and as you're a refugee from Missouri, I kind o' feel a feller-feelin' for you; an' ef you've no objections, I'm powerful weak and hungry, and wouldn't care to have a little morsel to eat."

"Certainly,— most certainly, my friend," replied the parson; "though poor, we still have something to satisfy hunger."

Mrs. Southdown by this time was on her feet, and making the dishes rattle. Ludicrous as the poor fellow's story was, it had touched a tender chord in her heart and awakened the liveliest sympathies.

"I was so hungry," resumed the refugee, "that I stopped on the road a mile or so back, an' tried to git some dinner. When I tole 'em I wus druve out of Missouri, they said, says they, 'You must a-been an abolitionist, or you wouldn't 'ave been druve off that way.' Now, ye see, that kind o' riled me all over, 'case I jist as live be called a hos-thief as an abolitionist. One a'n't no better 'an tother. I've alers been furnents abolition, ever sense I wus borned. So them folks told me I might go amongst the

Black Republicans to git my dinner. Well, ye see, the more I denied bein' an abolitionist, the more they stuck to it I wus. Plague take sich a set! I wus mad enough to 'ave fout 'em."

"You will find plenty of such people in this country," responded the parson.

"They'd better mind how they 'cuse me of bein' an abolitionist," continued the fellow; "nothin' riles me like that. An' spacially when I'm parted from my pracious wife an' children. Oh, jist to think of it! how this awful war's separatin' husban' an' wife, parents an' children, brothers an' sisters! Oh, it's shockin' to human natur!"

"True, that is very hard, my friend," observed Parson Southdown; "but, after all, some good may come of it. Some of us need to be taught what it is to be separated from nearest and dearest friends. I have met with a great many slave-holders in this State and Iowa, who, for their love of the Union, had to fly from Missouri and Arkansas; they make a wonderful ado about being forced to separate from their friends; husbands complain of being sundered from their wives and children, and the wives and children left behind complain as bitterly, no doubt, that husband and father have been cruelly compelled to part from them. But let us only think of the infinitely more cruel separations that have been common and of daily occurrence at the South for generations. Mothers and fathers have been sold from their children; children sold from their parents; husbands sold from their wives, and wives from their husbands, — and parted, in many instances, forever. Yet all that is thought nothing of."

"Case why! they are niggers," said the refugee.

"That makes it none the less cruel and unjust," responded the parson; "they have feeling and affection the same as we have."

"S'pose they have, a'n't they niggers?"

"Ah, I perceive you have the unanswerable, stereotyped, pro-slavery argument. They are niggers; that's what confounds us. And it is the sum and substance of all the arguments used by the champions of slavery, North and South. The argument is formidable and irrefut-

able, simply because it is pointless and sense-
less; to refute it would be to refute an empty
sound."

" I don't boast of havin' no great larnin', but
I'm edecated enough to know that niggers wur
made fur slaves."

" But let us go back to this complaint you
make about being separated from your wife and
children. You do not expect this separation to
last; when the war is over, if not sooner, you
expect to return to your home and family. I
have seen slave-fathers, of as fine feelings, and
as warm affections as yourself, and no less intelligent, sold in Missouri, and taken to Alabama
and Louisiana, and elsewhere in the South, —
taken from wife and children without the proba-
bility or hope of ever meeting again in this
world. The friends of slavery, who are now
scattered and sundered, through the operations
of civil war, should think of the thousands and
tens of thousands of poor slaves, who have been
treated as if they were beasts, incapable of
feeling and affection, — and they should think
of the parents and children, husbands and wives,

they themselves have been the means of parting forever."

" Well, raily! Shor'es my name's Piper, I
never in all my born days hurn anybody talk
up for niggers that way."

At this juncture, a mulatto man rapped at the
threshold.

" Walk in," said the parson, rising and offering
a chair to the stranger.

" Excuse me, sir," said the colored man, timid-
ly; "I am travelling, and am without money;
though not accustomed to beg, I am compelled
to ask for something to eat."

" Please be seated, sir," answered the parson;
" you will be welcome to such as we have."

" Whur you from, and whur are you gwien
to ?" impertinently demanded Piper.

" I am from the State of Missouri, sir," replied
the mulatto, civilly, yet in a tone of rebuke.
Manifestly, he at once perceived that the ques-
tioner was an impertinent clown.

" I guess you're a runaway slave," persisted
Piper, in his impertinence.

" I have been a slave, sir," said the fugitive,

frankly; "but Fortune's wheel, which now low-ers the proud oppressor, has elevated me. And I hope, before it's done turning, it will raise and make free all my down-trodden race."

"Hi ho! you talk as impudent as any free nigger I ever come across. I 'spect you cal-kilate on doin' big things in this free country. You'd be enough sight better off with your moster."

"My place is vacant, sir; if you think it a desirable situation, you shall be quite welcome to it."

"I a'n't a nigger."

"There are plenty of slaves whiter than you, sir."

By this time dinner was ready, and the hungry men were both invited to take seats at the table. Piper rushed forward, and, seating himself, seized his knife and fork, and went to work like a starved hound. The fugitive modestly approached the table, and was about to take a seat, when Piper said,—

"I guess you'll wait till I'm done."

"I've no predjudice against color, sir," replied the mulatto, with a mischievous twinkle in his eye. Yet he hesitated a moment; but as soon as he glanced at Mrs. Southdown, he perceived he had her approbation, which was all he wanted, and proceeded to take a seat at the table.

"Get away from here, you impudent nigger!" bawled Piper, in the most ruffian-like manner.

"If you expect to eat at my table, sir," said the parson, "you must conduct yourself more like a gentleman."

"I wusn't fotch up to eat with slaves; and I'm not gwien to be imposed on."

"If I've imposed on anybody, it's upon this colored gentleman, in asking him to eat with such a scavenger-looking fellow as you."

Jumping up from the table in a rage, Piper began walking the floor to and fro, puffing and blowing considerably.

Now Mrs. Southdown brought in a dish of nice fried ham and eggs, and set it before the fugitive. To this new dish Piper's longing eyes turned wistfully. There was now a struggle between appetite and dignity; between pride and an empty stomach. The fugitive observed this internal conflict, and secretly hoped that pride would prevail; but very soon he perceived that ravenous appetite was about to gain the ascendency; as Piper sullenly drew up to the table, the contraband appropriated the ham and eggs by sweeping the contents of the dish into his own plate. At this, Piper looked daggers, and could hardly restrain himself from going into another diabolical rage; but he wisely concluded to fill his mouth with cabbage rather than angry words. After all, he made a hearty meal; but got no ham and eggs.

Ascertaining that the fugitive slave had been in the habit of preaching occasionally to his fellow-bondmen, Parson Southdown proposed that he should make a public discourse to the citizens of the village, on slavery and the rebellion; to which he consented. The appointment was made; and when the time came round, a great crowd convened to hear him. More were there, however, from bad intent than from good motives.

With simple, but impressive and touching, eloquence, the fugitive pleaded the cause of his ignored and persecuted race. In the midst of his powerful appeals, an Irishman, standing in the crowd, cried out, "Oh, wonderful! who ever heard the leik from a nager!"

"Poh!" said a tory, standing near him, — "Flanna O'Larkin, don't be humbugged by that fellow; he's only half nigger."

"Only half nager, ond can do sooch woonders! by jabers, what thin could he do af he were all nager?"

At the conclusion of his speech, a copperhead politician said to his clan, in a loud voice, that he guessed the fugitive slave law was still in force, and that, being a law-abiding man, he felt disposed, if he could get assistance, to return this runaway slave to his master.

A score or more of the baser sort at once rallied round the politician, proffering to assist him in taking the negro. Parson Southdown, anticipating the possibility of such a demonstration, had slipped a couple of revolvers into his pocket.

"This man is my guest," said the parson; "I will protect him at the risk of my life."

The politician, with a gang of villains at his heels, made at the fugitive. But luckily, Parson Southdown was already between the parties; quickly drawing his revolvers, and taking one in each hand, he declared his intention to kill as many of them as he could. The wretches stood back.

The mob soon dispersed, but evidently with the intention of arming themselves, the more safely to carry out their villanous designs.

There happened to be an officer present, who had a company of new recruits encamped within a few miles of the place. Seeing that the mob was bent on violence, he hastened back to camp, and speedily as possible brought his men into the copperhead village, and just in time to quell what, evidently, would have proved a serious riot. The mob had surrounded Parson Southdown's domicile, threatening violence if the negro was not given up. Not knowing that there were any Federal soldiers in the neighborhood, the ruffians were taken greatly by surprise when they found themselves surrounded by armed men.

The captain of the company arrested the whole tatterdemalion crew, and kept them under guard two days, allowing them only bread and water for their rations. During which time, the parson took his family and the fugitive to an adjoining county, where there was more loyalty, and a better and more intelligent class of people.

The day after the parson's removal to his new home, lo! and who should make his appearance but Uncle Ned of Platte City.

"Ho, ho! Massa Soufdown," cried the good old darky, while .his faded and sunken eyes kindled and sparkled with new life and fire; "ho, ho! I's kotch up wid you at last!"

"Bless your soul, Uncle Ned!" exclaimed the parson; "what in the world has brought you here?"

"Why, dese free legs; praise be to de good Lor A'mighty!"

"Pray, what's happened, Uncle Ned?" said Mrs.

Southdown, clasping the old man's hand with ecstasy.

" Why, de yur ob jubelo am come !" answered he ; "but de rebels, dey say de Debil's to pay. So, as dis darky don't owe dat ole chap nufin, he leave de secesh to foot de bill, while he footed up de hill an down de valley."

" But how did you get away ?"

" Why, you see de Union soldiers come dare one day mighty onexpected, an massa — dat is to say, him dat wus my massa, — took a mighty skur, an runs like a wile turkey gobbler. I kind o' spect he's gwien yit; an ef de good Lord please, may de Debil help 'im on! He's gwien de right course."

" Which way did he travel ?"

" Right straight for Arkansaw. I'm shore de bad place a'n't fur from dar. Den thinks I, ef massa's gwien Souf, I'se gwien Norf, an' de more miles we put 'tween us de better."

" And how did you manage to find out where we lived ? "

" You see, I stops las' night at a tavern, an' I overhurs 'em talkin' 'bout some abolition preacher. Den I 'quires ef his name wur Soufdown.

'I 'blieve dat's what da call de rascal,' say de lan'lord. Den, thinks I, de good Lord have been guidin' my poor feet de right way. So I keeps on 'quirin' till I fin's you, thank de Lor' A'mighty."

"And how do you like this free country, Uncle Ned ?"

" Oh, I likes de country, case it's de land ob freedom ; an' I likes de air ; it smack ob liberty, an' smell ob de blossoms ob freedom. But dis darky kind o' don't like de peoples 'bout hur ; da ar' too much like de white trash down Souf. Da most all am gwien in for secesh. One gentman at de tavern called 'em copperheads. Now, dat's jist de bestest name I knows ob for dem. I's 'quainted wid dat snake, what da call copperhead ; 'tis de meanest snake dat eber crawled. Its head am flat, an' jist de color ob a new copper cent. An' den it's so sly dat you neber sees him till he bites you. An nuffin's pisiner dan de bite ob de copperhead. Now, dese ar' secesh in dis land ob freedom belong to de same generation ob serpents. An' it's mighty easy to tell who da ar', when ye gits de nack ob it. I knows dese copperheads politicianers from de wink ob de eye. All dem ar' kind ob men what foller de blackleg business, an' hos-racin' an' gittin' drunk, and sich like thing, am de copper-head', ebery one ob dem."

"How are the people doing at Platte City, Uncle Ned?" inquired Mrs. Southdown.

"Da ar' all gwien to de Debil fast as da kin. De slave-holders am allers talkin' 'bout dar rights; neber mind; I tells ye, da'll git dar rights one ob dese days, when de Ole Boy flies 'way wid 'em. Da'll fin' out dat ole Hornie hab some rights, too."

"It's hard to tell, Uncle Ned, what will become of them," remarked the parson.

"I s'pose de good Book don't say nuffin' 'bout dem; but it tells what come ob some rebels jist like 'em. Da say dar wus a rebellion in heben once. De secesh angels, widout any cause, jist like de secesh at de Souf, not bearin' in mind dat da had all dat heart could wish, an' plenty ob glory, still all dat didn't satisfy 'em; da kicked up a muss, jist like Souf Carliner; den we see what follered; da wur all tumbled out ob heben

into dat deep pit what hab no bottom.   Da wur·
nine days fallin' afore da reached de lake ob fire
an' brimstone.   Now, dat's what come ob de
fust rebels, Massa Soufdown."

.   .   .   .

After the flower of the country, from every
section throughout the State of Illinois, had left
their homes to give their lives, if need be, for
the life of the nation, the disloyal men of the
State, finding themselves in the majority, grew
bold in their treason, and ever since have done
all within their power to hinder the putting
down of the rebellion.

22*

CHAPTER XX.

"Thoughts shut up want air,
And spoil like bales unopened to the sun."

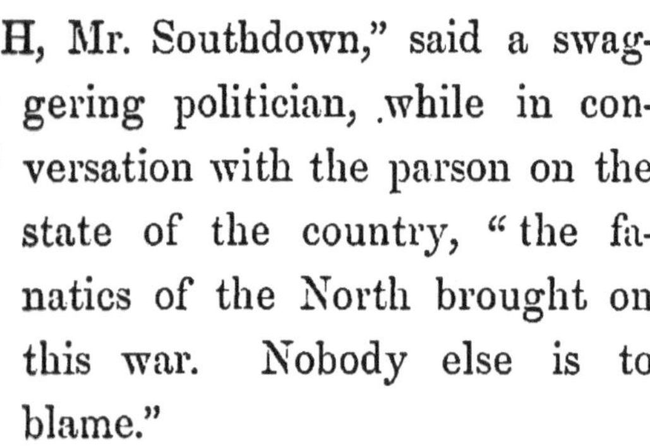

H, Mr. Southdown," said a swaggering politician, while in conversation with the parson on the state of the country, "the fanatics of the North brought on this war. Nobody else is to blame."

"And do you state that for a fact, Mr. Squib ?"

"Of course I do, sir ; a notorious fact."

"Did the fanatics of the North begin the war ?"

"They began the agitation of the slavery question, which led, as I always knew it would, to civil war. The fact is, sir, the South has been shamefully imposed upon ; the rights of the slave-holder have been disregarded. The Southern States have good reason for breaking up the Union and throwing off the iron yoke of the old Yankee government."

"Such being not only your own sentiments, Mr. Squib, but also the teaching of your party, I beg leave to call your attention to a few declarations made by Alexander H. Stephens, Vice President of the Southern Confederacy, on the floor of the convention called to vote Georgia out of the Union."

"What care I for what Stephens said?"

"He is a Southern man, and a secessionist, and, besides, one of their very brightest, best, and most influential men. His opinions, therefore, touching national affairs, and especially Southern rights, ought certainly to be entitled to some weight."

"It is enough for me to know that the Southern States have been robbed of their rights, and that the abolitionists have been the cause of the war."

"But hear what this Southern statesman says to a convention of slave-holders : —

"'This step once taken can never be recalled,' — I give you his exact words, — 'and all the baleful and withering consequences that must follow will rest on the convention for all coming time.

"'When we and our posterity,' said he 'shall see our lovely South desolated by the demon of war, which this act of yours will inevitably call forth, when our green fields and waving harvests shall be trodden down, and all the horrors and desolations of civil war upon us, — who but this convention will be responsible for it? And who but he who shall have given his vote for this unwise and ill-timed measure shall be held to strict account for this suicidal act by the present generation, and cursed and execrated by posterity for all coming time?

"'Pause, I entreat you,' continued he, with all the energy and in all the earnestness of his soul, 'and consider, for a moment, what reasons you can give to your fellow-sufferers in the calamity that it will bring upon us? What reason can you give to the nations of the earth to justify it? To what cause can you point, or what single overt act can you name, on which to rest the plea of justification? What right has the North assailed? What interest of the South has been invaded? What justice has been denied? And what claim, founded in justice and right, has been withheld?'"

"Well, well, what did all that signify?" demanded the politician, contemptuously.

"A great deal," responded Southdown; "and further, said Mr. Stephens, 'Can either of you, to-day, name one governmental act of wrong, deliberately and purposely done by the government at Washington, of which the South has a right to complain? I challenge the answer!'"

"If I'd been there, I could have answered him," said the conceited blockhead.

"Then you could have done more than any member of the Georgia convention felt competent to do; for not one among them attempted to answer him, notwithstanding his bold challenge. But hear him still further; I have a distinct recollection, not only of the general drift and scope of his argument, but also of his very words: 'While on the other hand,' said he, 'let me show the facts. You know, gentlemen, I am not here the advocate of the North; but I am here the friend,—the firm friend and lover of the South; and for this reason I speak thus plainly, uttering only words of truth and soberness. Let me, then, state a few facts which are clear and undeniable, and which now stand as records authentic in the history of our country.

"'When we demanded the slave-trade, or the importation of Africans for the cultivation of our lands, did they not yield the right for twenty years? When we asked and demanded the return of our fugitive slaves, was it not granted in the passage of the fugitive slave law of 1850?

"'Whatever individuals may have done, the government has always been true to Southern interests.'"

"Ah, but he wouldn't say that now," remarked the politician, ill-naturedly.

" I presume not, indeed, for he has since been bought over to secession. The offer of the Vice Presidency was too great a temptation.

He has sold himself to the Devil, just as all you traitors have."

"Intend you to insult me, sir?"

"The honest truth should insult no man. But let me tell you something more of what Mr. Stephens said on the floor of the Georgia convention.

"'Look,' said he, 'at another fact: when we have asked that more territory should be added, that we might spread the institution of slavery, have they not yielded to our demands in giving us Louisiana, Florida, and Texas, out of which four States have been carved, and ample territory for four more to be added in due time, if you by this mad act do not destroy this hope, and perhaps by it, lose all, and have your last slave wrenched from you by stern military rule, or by a decree of universal emancipation, which may reasonably be expected to follow?'"

"Did he say that?" demanded the politician, looking surprised.

"Such were his words; and how prophetic! I must give you still more of his language:—

"'What have we to gain,' said he, 'by this

proposed change of our relation to the general government?   We have always had the control of it, and can yet if we remain in it and are as united as we have been.

"'We have had a majority of the presidents chosen from the South, as well as the control and management of most of those chosen from the North.'

"In making these declarations, Mr. Stephens but stated plain, obvious facts, which every well-read man in the history of his country ought to know."

In reply to this, the politician commenced cursing the abolitionists and eulogizing the institution of slavery.

"All our great and good men," remarked the parson, "have uniformly regarded slavery as depraving in its tendency; calculated to blight the heart and darken the mind.   I remember Mr. Jefferson says, in his Notes on Virginia:—

"'There must, doubtless, be an unhappy influence on the manners of our people, produced by the existence of slavery among us.   The whole commerce between master and slave is a perpetual exercise of the most boisterous passions, — the most unrelenting despotism on the one part, and degrading submission on the other. Our children see this and learn to imitate it. The parent storms; the child looks on, catches the lineaments of wrath, puts on the same airs in the circle of smaller slaves, gives a loose rein to the worst passions, and thus nursed, educated, and daily exercised in tyranny, cannot but be stamped by it with odious peculiarities. The man must be a prodigy who can retain his manners and morals undepraved by such circumstances.'"

"Poh! poh!" said the politician. "Tom Jefferson was a visionary man; full of new ideas and strange theories that nobody but himself ever believed."

"As to the vitiating tendency of slavery, Mr. Madison was of the same opinion. I can give you his language upon that very point, — at least, a sentence : —

"'Let us save our country,' said he, 'from reproaches, and our posterity from the imbecility ever attendant on a country filled with slaves.'

"And the great-minded Patrick Henry holds language still stronger : —

" ' Is it not a little surprising,' says he, ' that professors of Christianity, whose chief excellence consists in softening the human heart, in cherishing and improving its finer feelings, should encourage a practice so totally repugnant to the first impressions of right and wrong ? '

" Washington expressed similar opinions, and evidently was fully persuaded in his own mind that slavery was destined to be speedily abolished."

"And these very men you summon as witnesses against slavery, themselves held slaves."

"Ah, but do you not perceive that that very circumstance gives the more weight to their testimony? It was but yesterday I heard you say that the rabid Northern abolitionists would all be in favor of slavery if they owned slaves. Their testimony has no weight with you because they have no interest in the institution. Jefferson, Madison, Henry, and Washington are set aside by you because they had an interest in the institution. The sincerity of these great statesmen is the clearer, since their testimony went against their own interest.

" Besides, there was an apology, and there still is an apology, for a good man's owning slaves until the black laws are changed or the institution abolished. Both the Slave States and a number of the Free States have laws that oppress and work great injustice to free blacks. Illinois and Indiana are sadly disgraced by their black laws.

" But a few years ago, a drunken legislative body in Missouri passed an act reducing to slavery all free negroes who did not leave the State within a given time. It was known to that body, at the same time, that the adjoining Free States had laws that prohibited free colored people from coming within their borders. But for the magnanimity of the then governor of Missouri, who vetoed the bill, the free negroes of the State would have had no alternative but slavery.

" The men who composed that legislative body should have been born in the dark ages, when humanity was lost in brutality.

"But a word more in reference to the institution you so much admire. Only compare the Northern States with the Southern. How striking is the contrast! What has made the difference? This is a question that needs no answer. In the pestilential atmosphere of slavery nothing succeeds; progress and prosperity are unknown; supineness and slothfulness ensue; wretchedness and desolation run riot throughout the land, and an aspect of most melancholy inactivity and dilapidation broods over every city and town; ignorance and prejudice sit enthroned over the minds of the people; usurping despots wield the sceptre of power;—everywhere and in everything, throughout the South, the multitudinous evils of slavery are apparent.

"Going from the South to the North, we see the condemnation of slavery written upon everything,—improvements, inventions, and whatever displays enterprise, taste, genius;—ay, and literature, learning, science, and philosophy, at the North, all rise up to condemn slavery."

But the parson was again casting pearl before swine. Words of truth and wisdom are thrown away when addressed to men who love falsehood and are wedded to folly.

How little the politician profited by the reasoning of Rev. Southdown may be seen in the following incident, which happened but a few hours after his conversation with the parson: —

A man of silvery hair, and bearing many a scar, had just returned from the war. He sat with his head bowed in sorrow, and leaning upon his staff; his wife and children were weeping around him; for he had brought back, not only a mutilated body, but the sad intelligence that his youngest son had fallen in battle.

In the midst of this touching scene, the politician came in, and, abruptly addressing the weary, heart-stricken soldier, said, —

"Well, old man, you are back, it seems, from the abolition war, and minus an arm I perceive, and got a few awkward hacks and ugly scratches, besides. The chivalry must have been after you right sharp when you got that frightful gash on the side of your face. Ha, ha! I reckon you're beginning to find out that fighting for niggers don't pay. And I understand you got one of your boys killed down there. Don't you think you'd both been better off at home, eh?"

The soldier slowly raised his drooping head, wiped the tears from his bronzed and furrowed cheek, bent a look of proud scorn and manly indignation upon the pusillanimous wretch who stood before him; then, rising deliberately to his feet, said, —

"True, sir, I have lost a son in the bloody conflict, and, in addition to receiving many wounds, have lost an arm; but, rather than be a traitor, or have any one near and dear to me play a traitor's part, I would freely lose another arm and another son, and be covered with wounds and bruises from the crown of my head to the soles of my feet! We live not for self alone; we owe duties to God, to humanity, and to our country; we owe duties to posterity. This war is not for the present generation only; it is for unborn millions; it is for the perpetuity of a republican form of government, the perpetuity of our free institutions; it is a

war against despotism and oppression; it is a
war against a race of petty tyrants who glory
in loading with chains both the minds and the
bodies of men; it is a war for the upholding of
a great government, and the suppression of the
most causeless and diabolical rebellion ever
known upon the face of the earth. There have
been justifiable rebellions,—rebellions against
tyranny, and for progress and liberty; but this
is a rebellion to turn the tide of progress backward, and to crush the very spirit of liberty.

"When I think what is at stake in this war,
and consider the imperilled condition of the
government, and when I call to mind the sacrifices that loyal men are making for their country, and knowing at the same time, as I do, that
the struggle is being prolonged, the war pro-
tracted, and the terrible conflict made more sanguinary, by the encouragement which disloyal
men here at home are giving armed traitors at
the South,—when I *think* of these things," repeated the gray-haired soldier, while the fires of
true patriotism and a just indignation kindled
in his noble eye, "and remember," continued he,

"what toils and suffering our patriotic brethren are enduring, separated from their families and homes, and constantly in the midst of danger and death, and then listen to the pratings of such contemptible tories as you, who have willingly done nothing for your country, while you enjoy the protection of its laws, I must confess it stirs my blood,—at least, what little I have left.   Thank God, I have one arm yet; and with that I perhaps cannot serve my country better than by breaking the pate of a copperhead;" and whack! he struck the intruder with his cane, making a telling impression upon a skull which arguments had been hurled at in vain. "Take that, you serpent!" said he,—"and that! you vile traitor!" hitting him again,—"and that, you unhung tory!" whacking him over the head a third time.   The last blow brought the impertinent politician to the floor, lustily crying for quarter.

CHAPTER XXI.

"First a shadow, then a sorrow
Till the air is dark with anguish."

ELL, parson," said an avowed infidel to Southdown, "you are a believer in a divine providence; tell me how you reconcile your doctrine with this war, and the distress, calamities, and bloodshed it is causing."

"While I believe in a divine providence, Mr. Dudley," replied the parson, "I also believe in free moral ability; or, in other words, that man is a free agent, having power to do good or evil, — and destined, under God's overruling providence to take the consequences. In the abuse of their free agency, evil-minded men have brought this great trouble upon the country."

"But why did not God, in his providence, prevent the dire results which have grown out of their treasonable acts? Without interfering with their free agency, could he not have turned aside the fatal blow, and saved us from bloody strife, and the sunny South from desolation?"

"Unquestionably; but we must take into consideration the fact that we had become a very wicked nation,—and besides, that we have long cherished, and still are fostering in the bosom of the nation, a most wicked institution,—a system of injustice and oppression, which is utterly incompatible with Christianity, and a vile abomination in the sight of God."

"Ah, but how does that help your side of the question?"

"Thus: we need humbling; and God sees that nothing but fearful national calamities, sorrow, and suffering, will answer the purpose, bring down our pride and beget a spirit of repentance that will work reformation. Therefore, he has permitted us to bring upon ourselves the terrible scourge of civil war; and, while we deserve all we are suffering, and tenfold more, yet I doubt not, that in God's providence it will be for the nation's greatest good in the end. However blind we may be to it, future generations will clearly see the hand of God in this war. And while they may bedew with tears the pages of history that shall tell of our sufferings, yet they will perceive that no milder remedy could have saved us."

"At the present crisis, there appears to my mind a better prospect for being destroyed than saved. The remedy is likely to be worse than the malady."

"The whole head is sick, and the whole heart is faint; there is no soundness in the nation. And, worst of all, we are unwilling to acknowledge the desperate state we are in, and to confess we need a remedy. Sordid interest stands in the way of justice and humanity; yet man-ifestly Heaven intends that oppression shall cease; and, if nothing but war and desolation can break the tyrant's power and strike the chains of slavery from the limbs of the bondman, why, then war and desolation must come."

"I cannot see that we deserve such a scourge, or that we are so great sinners after all."

"No nation, perhaps, has been blessed like ours; and none has been more ungraceful. Just before the dark and stormy night of disunion and civil war gathered over us, we were glorying in our strength, and boasting of our wisdom, wealth, and prosperity. We thought 'the race was to the swift and the battle to the strong;' and we had forgotten the divine declaration, ' *Righteousness* exalteth a nation.' Contemning the weak, and despising the poor and helpless, we delighted in tyranny, cruelty, and oppression. Ignoring the higher law, and disregarding Heaven's plainest mandates, we trampled down truth, justice, and mercy."

"In these respects, have we been worse than other nations?"

"We have been worse, in that we have been more highly favored. Looking over our broad land, contemplating its vastness and its immense resources, and considering the rapid strides it had made and was making in wealth and power, — surveying its rich valleys and its golden mountains, its fruitful fields and its exhaustless mines, we grew proud, haughty, and ungrateful, even insolent and defiant. We almost ceased to fear God or to regard man; and said in our hearts, 'Who shall try swords with such a nation as this? or, who presume to measure arms with these United States?'"

"I grant you, we have been too boastful."

"Ay; pluming ourselves upon national greatness, we dreamed not that there was weakness in our strength. Nor remembered the proverb, 'A haughty spirit goeth before a fall.' Heaven ordains that the high-headed and stiff-necked shall be brought low; and that the pride of nations, as well as of individuals, shall be humbled."

"Be that as it may, the American people are now in a fair way to experience humility."

"Yes; she that boasteth herself 'the queen of the world and the child of the skies' is destined to come down and sit in the dust. Already, distraction and dismay have suddenly taken the place of peace and prosperity. Our sun went down at noon; and an appalling night is now upon us, — an almost rayless, moonless, starless, night! The nation's sky is overcast by tempest clouds of frightful aspect, through which grim-visaged War with desperate fury drives his fiery steeds and gory chariot."

"Yet how hard to realize that it is so,— to realize that war is raging, and that bloody battles are being fought in our own country,— our once happy country, so long accustomed to peace."

"True; it almost staggers belief; especially when we think of the magnitude and extent of the conflict, having a sweep of scarcely less than ten thousand miles. Only let your mind's eye range the length and breadth of our ensanguined plains, — almost the entire land of slavery may be regarded as one great field of battle. In the world's history such a battle-field never before was known."

"Alas! what desolation is being wrought! Oh the blood and treasure it has already cost!"

"'Tis fearful to think of. But that it is so, why should we marvel? Is there not a God of justice? Can we be surprised at his righteous judgments? Is it strange that a day of reckoning has at last come?"

"If it be a providence, I must confess that to me it is a mysterious, inexplicable providence."

"Why should we marvel that the Almighty, in righteous indignation, has allowed the wicked men, whom the people, in their blindness and perverseness, so long exalted to power, to kindle a consuming fire in the bosom of the nation?"

"That may be orthodox theology, but, to my mind, it is utterly incomprehensible."

"Just Heaven sometimes makes use of wicked men to scourge the wicked."

"Why, then, is it not done in all cases, and more thoroughly?"

"God's dealings with men must necessarily be such as not to interfere with their free moral ability. If the Almighty governed the moral world as he does the physical, by laws of force and stern necessity, then would man be robbed of his most exalted attributes and highest honor, — free-will, power of choice, responsibility; he would be nothing more than a machine, and no more accountable for his conduct than the rivers, the tides, the winds, the clouds."

"It seems to me that finite, erring man is an

object of pity and commiseration rather than of blame and animadversion. He is limited in knowledge, weak in his faculties, and blinded by his passions. Temptation assails him, and he has no power to resist its force; evil comes upon him, and he foresees it not. Who is wise enough to have anticipated our present trouble? It came like the sudden bursting of a tempest upon the land, or a startling thunder-peal to the unsheltered traveller, when he thought the sky was clear."

"Ah, but not exactly so. For more than a generation this storm was brewing. Low mutterings, thunders, were long heard in the distance, and frowning clouds, for years, hung darkly about our national horizon; but a crooked and perverse generation was strangely blind and deaf to the warning."

" Perhaps strangely, but not culpably, blind and deaf?"

" Yes, culpably; for we would not believe ourselves in danger, though sages foretold and statesmen predicted — long predicted — disaster to the country and the coming of national earth-

quakes, whirlwinds, and tempests. It was only
the wilfully and stubbornly blind who could not .
see years ago the foreshadowing of our present
trouble and national distress."

" To be sure, we have had political prophets,
fanatics, and alarmists, but we believed them
not."

" We should at least have heeded the signs of
the times, paused in our mad career, and called
upon God to save us from our national sins. But,
'On with the dance!' said a million voices;
'let joy be unconfined!' President and cabinet,
senators and representatives, led in the giddy
whirl, while the upper-ten and lower-million followed in their wake. Washington City spent
the day and shared the night in banqueting,
revelry, and dissipation; ay, and in vile debauch
and lewd wantonness."

"A bad set they were there, in Pierce's time
and through Buchanan's reign. The old dotard,
and his more treacherous predecessor, committed
sin enough to damn a nation."

" Moral pestilence, as well as physical, is con-
tagious; almost all the cities in the land, copy-

ing the example of the Federal capital, did, nearly
as they could, the same things that were done
at Washington. For many years prior, and up
to the time of this nightfall upon the nation,
we have had, especially in political circles and
amongst our office-holders, all over the length
and breadth of the land, disgraceful profligacy,
miserable demagoguism, villanous plots, coffee-
house caucusing, wire-working, trickery, and
secret conclaves, where conspiracies, knavery,
and all kinds of treasonable schemes and dark
designs have been carried on."

"I fain would persuade myself, parson, that
your imagination has colored the picture;
yet I must own that recent developments have
proved to me that the class of men you speak
of, and especially the disloyal wretches who,
while in office, were plotting treason against the
government they were pretending to serve, are
even worse — more heartless and treacherous
than language can describe."

" Besides, among such men, party rancor has
known no bounds; truth and honesty have been
laughed at, while cunning intrigue and shrewd

rascality were praised. Political corruption has been rife; principle accounted nothing; party, everything. The perpetual aim of demagogues has been to keep the political furnace red-hot, by blowing the bellows of party, and fanning the flames of passion. A professional politician cares not whose house gets on fire, so his own pot boils."

"Alas for any country in which dishonesty is rewarded! For then integrity, truth, and virtue retire in disgust from the public walks of life."

"Ay; leaving rogues and traitors to manage the affairs of the government. And I must own, however much it may reflect upon my own profession, that dishonesty, in many sections, has been scarcely less rewarded in Church than in State. Hence, time-serving incumbents of the pulpit, as well as office-seekers, have lent themselves to the cause of injustice, aristocracy, and oppression.

"With this state of things long existing, and constantly growing worse, what could we have expected? — what but that our national sky

would gather blackness and tempest, and pour
down upon our heads a deluge of wrath?

"After a long forbearance, is it strange that
divine vengeance has at last kindled to a devouring flame? Is it strange that fire and sword
are now doing their fearful work of slaughter
and devastation in the fairest portion of our
guilty land?

" Through the wicked persistency of the slave-
driving tyrants who inaugurated civil war for
the purpose of augmenting their despotic power,
the soil of every slave-holding State has already
been drenched with blood, and its rivers made red
by the purple tide of the slain. And still the din
of arms is heard above the groans of the dying
and the wail of the widow and the orphan?
While the nation has been ripening for this
dreadful scourge, while sin has been added to
sin, iniquity heaped on iniquity, and while the
enemies of the Union and the foes of freedom
have been hatching their foul treason and diabolical conspiracies, Zion's watchmen, as well
as our statesmen, for the most part, have slept !
— slept, or waking, cried, ' Peace ! peace ! when
there was no peace.'

" True, indeed, a few faithful men there were, who, lifting up their voices, cried aloud in the ears of all the people, warning them of the coming storm, warning them of the nearness of a day of retribution and an impending revelation of wrath and fiery indignation that should sweep as a whirlwind, overwhelming the proud, the wicked, and the oppressor. And these true and faithful men were bitterly denounced as false prophets, fanatics, and agitators, who deserved only scorn, derision, persecution, or the gibbet; and not a few of their number, to the great disgrace of our boasted Republic, died martyrs to the cause of freedom, — were cruelly murdered by pro-slavery mobs, — and the government winked at it. Should we, therefore, complain when the vials of divine wrath are poured out upon so guilty a nation? Can we marvel at what is now befalling that portion of this great country desecrated by slavery, and where God is forgotten, religion made a mockery, and humanity outraged?

"A people clinging to an institution which is but the barbarous relic of a barbarous age, and that, in spite of the world's progress, and in the face of better light and knowledge, surely deserve the judgments and calamities that wilful blindness fails not, sooner or later, to bring.

" What are the woes which the slave-holders of the South are now suffering,—what the terror and despair that seize upon the heartless tyrants, but a just retribution for the magnitude of their sins, the blackness and enormity of their crimes ?   Profligacy, licentiousness, kidnapping, robbery, mobocracy, murder, and treason, are meeting with their appropriate rewards.   The day of vengeance — of terrible vengeance — has come !   Violence, carnage, and death wave their black banner in awful triumph where the slave, unpitied, so long clanked his chains."

"It seems retribution, indeed !   Nor can I say but what it is just."

" Divine justice and judgment never were more clearly seen than in the events now transpiring in the Slave States.   Only look at the sunny South, and see what is happening to the haughty, domineering chivalry of Dixie land ! Wild confusion, dire dismay and consternation, everywhere reign.   Treachery, distrust, and anarchy prevail; and starvation, too, will soon be at the threshold of the nabob as well as at the door of his menial, and in the cabin of his slave. Turn which way they will, the sword, pestilence, and famine stare the pampered chivalry in the face. Multitudes have already been smitten with iron hail; and their mangled bodies or bleaching bones lie scattered on hill and vale. Their fields are laid waste; their dwellings dismantled, and their ill-gotten gain, through unpaid toil, has taken to itself wings and flown."

"If the judgments of Heaven are to fall upon the Southern slave-holder, why should pro-slavery men of the North escape? Their principles are the same; they give countenance to the institution, and by their votes and voices help to uphold and perpetuate it."

"They will not escape; the curse of God is upon them, and his vengeance will sooner or later overtake them. In fact, they are already upon the rack, writhing under the mortification of defeat and the miscarriage of their treasonable plots. They plainly see, that unless they can break up the government, their political graves are dug."

CHAPTER XXII.

"'Mid cries and clashing arms, there came
The hollow sound of rushing flame!"

———

T was in Platte City, and on the 20th of August, 1863; the king of day was dipping behind the western hills, while his yellow locks still streamed out upon the horizon, burnishing as with gold a palace of clouds that hung in gorgeous splendor about him. At that hour a young man, with pale and thoughtful face, might have been seen on the summit of a green hill, a little way south of the village, poising a telescope, and looking toward the fast-declining sun; by his side stood a bright boy, perhaps somewhere in his teens. In the valley below, as the evening shades drew on. a company of horsemen made their appearance, and halted as if they had reached an appointed place of rendezvous. At the same time, in the village, hard by, there was hurrying to and fro, and with a slyness of movement calculated at once to awaken curiosity and suspicion. A noiseless but intense excitement prevailed ; men walked stealthily, and talked only in whispers ; while women sallied forth, ever and anon, here and there, and with white lips and trembling nerves inquired what was brewing. They were answered by mysterious looks, and with finger on the lip ; for a deed that night was to be done they dared not name ; ay, — such a deed, the very thought of which might turn the cheek of darkness pale.

A score or two of men, armed with guns, bowie-knives, and revolvers, in a very few minutes were mounted and moving off like a funeral procession, slowly and softly, in the direction of the valley, to the place of rendezvous.

Many citizens stared and wondered ; others looked wise, gave knowing winks, and nodded their heads significantly.

From various places along the border, similar bands set out about the same hour, and all, converging to one point, came together at midnight upon the banks of the Missouri River, where ample preparations had been made for a speedy crossing into Kansas.

We will here return, for a space, to our astronomer and his pupil, whom we left at eventide on the summit of the green hill adjacent to Platte City. The sun, which had made a golden set, was the object of their gaze till he sunk below the horizon and disappeared. Then, watching the stars as they came out one by one, and pointing their telescope to various quarters of the heavens, they viewed several of the planets and some of the fixed stars.

"Now, Alonzo," said the astronomer, "here, take a peep at Uranus through the telescope, — more commonly called Herschel. This planet was discovered in 1781 by Dr. William Herschel. It is eighty times larger than the earth."

"Eighty times the size of this world we're on, Mr. Lioni?" inquired the lad, in a tone of surprise and incredulity.

"Yes, eighty times."

"What a world it is!"

"Now let us lower the instrument a little, and take a view of Venus, — beautiful Venus, — the most brilliant of all the planets, and the second in order of distance from the sun. There, now, — that's a charming view."

"Oh, dear! It looks like the sun itself, Mr. Lioni."

"It is very bright. Let us swing round a little now, and get a glimpse of Saturn before that fleecy cloud gets over it. There's a world for you, my boy. You were surprised to hear me say that Herschel was eighty times larger than the earth; but what will you think when I tell you that Saturn is a thousand times larger?"

"A thousand times the size of the earth, Mr. Lioni? I declare! Well, well; I'm getting out of conceit with this little world of ours. Oh, I see that great belt, that glittering ring I've read about; how beautiful it looks!"

"Do you see any moons?"

"Moons? Oh, now I do! Two, — three!"

"There are eight; but you cannot see them all. It is growing somewhat late, and the air is a little chilly; we'll take a peep at Jupiter, and let that suffice for to-night. Jupiter is the largest planet in the solar system. It would make twelve hundred and eighty such worlds as this we inhabit."

"That almost staggers my power of belief, Mr. Lioni. Oh, it has a belt, too! That's grand!"

"Do you see any moons?"

"One, — yes, two."

"The other two are behind the planet."

"What's the reason our world couldn't have had a few more moons, Mr. Lioni?"

"Its rank among worlds is not of sufficient importance. The Creator has given us one more than we deserve, at any rate."

"Do you suppose the inhabitants of those great and beautiful worlds are better than the people here on this little planet?"

"If they are not, some huge comet ought to dash along, and knock them back into chaos."

"Do you think this world will ever get any better, Mr. Lioni?"

"It has taken a spell of getting worse lately. Yet I believe in progress, and look hopefully upon humanity, notwithstanding the vileness and brutality we have seen so much of lately. The heartless rebels, who are causing so much distress, are no worse in principle than they were in times of peace; they now find opportunity of giving full play to the savage disposition within them, which, before, was only held in check by the fear of punishment. From that class we have nothing to hope. Among reasoning men the car of progress is always advancing; but the unreflecting, human animals, who are governed only by their passions, are just where the vulgar herd were a thousand years ago. Outwardly they may seem superior to the barbarians and ignorant herds of past ages, and to be in advance of the heathen of our own time, but inwardly they are the same, the very same. The wild Indian, with his tomahawk and scalping-knife, never, to my knowledge, were guilty of anything more barbarous than what these rebel guerrillas are guilty of every day. Yet the wretches who compose our guerrilla bands are called civilized men; and, outwardly, as to form, feature, complexion, and apparel,

25*

seem to be such ; but that which makes a man
a savage is within him; and we can only tell
what is within the heart and mind of a man by
his acts. By this rule of judgment, we must
class a large number of our fellow-citizens with
heathen. Their conduct proves them unfit to
take rank even among ordinary savages; such
deeds as they commit would disgrace the most
warlike tribes of Indians. This ruffian band we
saw collecting in the valley, a little after sundown, I doubt not, has gone on a marauding expedition. God only knows how many innocent
people they may rob or murder before daylight. But enough of this now; let us go to
our respective lodgings. I will call at your room
to-morrow morning at about nine o'clock, and
give you another lesson in astronomy."

"If you please."

"I have nothing now to do; and it's some relief to my mind, these distressing times, to turn
aside to the quiet, peaceful paths of science;
and, if I can be of some use to you, my time
will not be thrown away."

"I shall be greatly indebted to you, Mr.
Lioni."

"The thought that I have been of some help to you in climbing the hill of science will amply reward me for any pains I may take. Good-night."

"Good-night, Mr. Lioni."

About the time the banditti crossed into Kansas, intelligence reached the Union troops at Kansas City, Mo., that Quantrell, with near a thousand Border-ruffians, was marching upon Lawrence, intending to murder the inhabitants, pillage and burn the town, and then proceed to Baldwin City and Prairie City, and treat them in the same way.

There were but three hundred Union soldiers at Kansas City; but, without a moment's delay, or the least hesitation, they mounted their horses and set out for Lawrence with all possible speed. Among these three hundred were Adrian Malvin, Parson Elmore, and Knickerbocker. But the cut-throats had too much the start; the soldiers were yet thirteen miles from Lawrence, when they saw the nocturnal heavens above the doomed village lighted with lurid flames.

This exciting scene, together with the thought of the terrible massacre, which they had reason to believe was going on, caused them to urge on their jaded horses to the utmost of their speed. Several noble animals fell dead, under their riders, on the way. Before the troops reached the burning town, the fiends had done their work of slaughter and robbery, and were on their way to Prairie City, robbing and burning as they went. The pursuing soldiers were able to follow in their track by the light of the burning buildings the miscreants fired on their way. Fortunately for Prairie City, Baldwin City, and other towns, which the vile wretches intended serving as they did Lawrence, the troops overtook and gave them battle. The banditti, however, stood the fire of the brave soldiers' but a few minutes. Leaving some twenty of their number on the ground, who were shot from their horses, they fled, still going in the direction of Prairie City. It was now daylight; and, as they neared the town they next expected to sack and burn, they discovered several hundred armed citizens advancing to meet them. At this they were seized with a panic, and fled in every direction. Many of them failed to make good their escape from Kansas; and those that succeeded in re-crossing the river were pursued into Missouri, and near a hundred of them killed.

What a scene Lawrence presented next morning to the face of day! . The great Free-State Hotel showed, among its smouldering ruins, embers, and ashes, many charred human bodies, while heaps of the dead lay in front of the smoking pile who had been shot while making their escape from the burning building. Amid the ashes of many private buildings, also, unconsumed portions of human bodies were to be seen, while dead men and boys, in their night-clothes, lay scattered up and down the streets, and over the Common, in every direction.

To look upon this horrid scene, and to see the crowds of distracted friends and relatives hunting out the marred and mangled forms of loved ones, and listen to the wail of mothers, sisters, wives, and children, were enough to move a heart of stone.

The actors in this shocking massacre, the

monsters who perpetrated the hellish crime, had mostly professed loyalty, and passed themselves at home for Union men ; and, besides, had generally taken the oath of allegiance to the Federal Government, thereby adding perjury and hypocrisy to barbarity and fiendish cruelty.

CHAPTER XXIII.

"'Tis the mind that makes the man."

OOD-MORNING, Alonzo! Now for another lesson in astronomy," said Lioni, entering the study of the lad who had spent a portion of the previous night with him upon the green hill viewing the planets through a telescope, and studying the laws that govern them.

"Good-morning, Mr. Lioni! I hope you didn't take cold last night, while trying to put new ideas into my dull brain."

"My blood's too hot, in these times of treason, violence, and foul murder, to be affected by a nipping air."

"Have you heard anything from the banditti we saw rendezvous in the valley last night?"

"Not a word yet. Indeed, I so dread to hear, that I have avoided speaking to any one on the street. I'm sure we are soon to have terrible tidings; I feel it all over me. But let us divert our minds from this painful subject, and talk about astronomy."

"My Uncle Thaddeus, from the country, called on me a little while this morning. He laughs at me about studying astronomy; says it's all ridiculous nonsense!"

"Oh, ho! poor old man! he'll never break his neck climbing amongst the stars, I dare say."

"He says, 'What's the use of it?'"

"Poh! a silly question. What's the use of anything? We may as well ask, What's the use of thinking? What's the use of living? What's the use of aspiring to aught above a brute?"

"He says if there are any other worlds than this, they are too far off to do us any good."

"I imagine he could take no interest in a world that's not likely to grow cabbage and potatoes for his own special benefit.

"Whatever elevates and happifies man, is of use, Alonzo. The study of astronomy exalts and sublimates our thoughts; enlarges, brightens, and invigorates our minds. Besides, while we gaze on the broad page of astronomical glory, we cannot but be impressed with a sense of the majesty, the power, wisdom, and goodness of the great Creator. While the study of astronomy unfolds the mind, it enlarges, chastens, and purifies the heart; makes us unselfish, promotes magnanimity of soul, and inspires generous and delicious sentiments. None but a supremely selfish man wants to believe that the world he inhabits is the chief part of creation and the centre of the universe, and that the sun, moon, and stars were created only for him and his race. Yet there are plenty of such men; they have no thought, care, nor sympathy for anything outside of themselves and the narrow circle in which they move. We see this exemplified right here in our midst; the people of Platte City think the cackle of their berg the bustle of the world! For them the earth stands, the sun shines, rises, and sets; for them the stars twinkle, and for them the Almighty sits upon the throne of the universe night and day."

"That makes me think of Elder Snooks's prayer, Mr. Lioni; he always prays as if he thought everything was made for him."

"No doubt he considers himself the but-end of all that God has made. The flea in his stocking might with much more reason say, This man was made for me. Parson Snooks's great wonder is, that the sun doesn't stand still when he preaches. When I heard him, — a sin I've been guilty of but once, — it seemed to me the sun of his knowledge was standing still, if not going back a little."

"I've not heard him often, except at a distance. He's gifted with a loud voice."

"So is your donkey. But, to change the subject, let me say to you, Alonzo, education makes as much difference between men as Nature has made between a man and a beast; even more. I have seen dogs that evinced more consideration, more refinement, more tenderness and affection, than many men."

"But are there not educated men, Mr. Lioni, who are very wicked?"

"Undeniably; but when I speak of the difference that education makes between men, I do not mean intellectual attainments merely; it is indispensable that moral culture and the education of the heart should be looked after. In the true sense of education, Alonzo, you will sometimes meet with men that cannot read, who are better educated than many of our scientific men. Not only better educated morally, but better educated intellectually; they reason more clearly, think more profoundly, comprehend principles and the various relations of things more readily. They have learned to exercise a common sense which anticipates the logic of the schools. I could tell you of slaves who have a much clearer perception of. moral principles and moral obligation than some of our learned divines. So you see, I mean by education the unfolding, brightening, and invigorating of our faculties, no matter how or where it is done, or whether with the aid of books and teachers or without them."

"I now understand you. Men may have learning without being thinkers."

"That is the great trouble; men do not think

enough, nor do they feel enough. Activity of thought and feeling intensifies life, and enhances the value of existence. Does that man truly live whose heart and brain have the nightmare? What to him is existence? Little better than a melancholy blank. What to him are the charms of science, the beauties and sublimities of nature, the glories of creation? To such men life has no significance, the universe no meaning. Ah, but this is not our lesson in astronomy."

"No matter, Mr. Lioni; I like to hear you talk on this subject of thinking."

"Well, then, I will dwell upon it a little longer; and let me impress you, Alonzo, especially, with the importance of mental industry and activity. While indolence weakens the intellect, it strengthens the passions; while it undermines virtue, it generates vice. The uncultured soul, like unploughed fields, brings forth that only which is vile, noxious, and unseemly. Inactivity cankers the mind, corrodes the heart, darkens and depraves all the powers of the soul; while industry and habitual exertion burnish the intellect, illumine the heart, vivify the affections, and invig-

orate the entire energies of our diviner nature.
Let me illustrate the thought I wish to fasten
upon you by a figure : you have seen the stagnant pool covered with its slimy scum, which
constantly breathes forth miasma to laden every
passing breeze with disease, pestilence, and death ;
you have also seen the crystal brook, whose
pure, bright waters go dancing merrily over beds
of white pebble ; you instinctively loathe the
stagnant pool, but delight to look upon the crystal brook. The former, being pent up, generates
noxious vapors, and becomes the abode of veno-
mous reptiles ; the latter, full of activity, and
leaping along its winding-way, is rendered pure,
healthful, musical, and beautiful. Do you get
my idea ? "

" Yes ; the idle mind is the stagnant pool."

" Ay ; in which vice hatches its miserable
brood. The active spirit " —

" Is the crystal brook."

"Ay ; gliding sweetly and cheerily over the
golden sands of life, reflecting celestial beauty,
and pouring the light of joy on all sides round."

" I like figures and comparisons; they make vivid and lasting impressions on my mind."

" Let me then amplify a little, in your favorite style, since you like it. We will compare a turbid, sluggish stream with the bounding, whirling, foaming cascade. The former has no charm for your eye, is altogether unbeautiful and unattractive. But how enchanting the latter!—rippling, gurgling to the brink, then, with a mighty leap, flinging its wild waves upon the silvery air to whiten in the wind."

"Ah, I see!"

" The turbid, sluggish stream is a fit type of the unthinking brain and unfeeling heart; while the sublime cascade, no less appropriately, typifies the active, energetic mind, busy thought, and the stirring, bounding soul."

"I see."

"Again; compare the dark waters of the Dead Sea with the rushing, thundering cataract of Niagara. The former presents a melancholy picture of death and desolation; the latter you gaze upon with ravished eyes and profoundest emotions of sublimity as it pours its eternal waters, with resistless force, from stupendous heights, adown frightful steeps, dashing against trembling rocks, turning dark huge waves to snow-white, feathery foam and clouds of winged spray that glitter in the sunlight with the inimitable hues of the rainbow. Now, there are human minds that, like the Dead Sea, present only a dismal picture of moral darkness and desolation ; while others remind you, in the might and majesty of their career, of that wonder in nature, the cataract of Niagara, whose bold, sweeping, booming, torrent awes creation round with its gigantic leap, deep-toned thunder, and earthquake-energy."

" Oh, I see ! "

"And what makes the striking difference between the Dead Sea and Niagara Falls ? "

"Activity."

" Yes ; motion, friction, velocity. What makes the difference between the minds of men ? "

"Activity."

" Yes ; action, energy, intensity. The proper and legitimate exercise of the mind develops strength, gives power and elasticity. Besides, action refines and beautifies in mind as well as in matter."

"I shall try to hold on to that idea, and make it profitable to me."

"Let me illustrate yet further: take a lump of gold from the mine; it is a shapeless mass, and has but little beauty to the eye; but now see it in the hands of the goldsmith, and watch the process of melting and working it; his fire and hammer directly change that shapeless mass to a glittering chain that is to encircle and adorn the neck of beauty. What a transformation! A yet greater and more wonderful transformation may, by proper influences and right appliances, be wrought on the human mind and heart."

"That gives me better light on the subject still."

"Just one more illustration, and I'll wind up. Take the rough diamond from its dark bed; it has to your eye but little indication of possessing qualities that give it rare value; but only wait till it is shaped and polished — what a polish! Now see it sparkle on the bosom of beauty, you begin to appreciate its qualities and estimate its worth. The undeveloped mind is the rough diamond, whose value does not yet appear; but wait till education does its work; wait until the bright images of truth, virtue, and religion are engraven on the tablets of the mind and heart, then see how the soul will shine!"

"Now we're going to be interrupted; yonder comes Parson Longface."

"Prodigious! Well, we may make up our minds to be bored without mercy, or else treat him uncivilly. He's the man who owns that crazy negro woman, isn't he?"

"Yes; he sold her child — a little, bright, yellow boy — to a man who lived in Alabama, and she went deranged about it. He treats her now very cruelly, they say."

"Yet he pretends to be a minister!"

A rap at the door now called Alonzo to his feet, who coolly invited the clergyman in and offered him a seat. Lioni frigidly bowed without rising.

"I am round collecting money for the Bible cause, and for missionary purposes," remarked

Parson Longface, gravely, and in long-drawn, solemn tones.

"I profess, parson," responded Lioni, "to be a friend to both the causes you mention; and have ever esteemed it a privilege to contribute something to aid in the good work of circulating the Scriptures among the destitute in our own country, and of sending the gospel to the heathen in foreign lands; but when solicited by *you* to contribute, either to the missionary or Bible cause, I find a serious difficulty in the way."

"How can that be?"

"While you profess to believe it necessary for men to read the Scriptures in order to obtain a knowledge of the way of life and salvation, you at the same time favor a system which deprives a large class of down-trodden people at home of the privilege of reading the Word of God."

"You mean the slaves, I suppose?"

"Yes; I mean the ignored and unfortunate race among us, whom we are so careful to keep in ignorance."

"Surely I had nothing to do in making the

laws that prohibit them from being taught to read."

"Are you not the man who entered complaint, at the last term of our circuit court, against one of our cleverest citizens, for teaching his slaves to read the Bible?"

" He was violating the law."

" And are you as careful to see that violations of the law are punished in other cases? One of your neighbors, and a member of your church, recently, while in a passion, mutilated one of his slaves in a most shocking manner, and in palpable violation of the law; yet no one thinks of entering complaint against him. That, I imagine, is not reckoned so serious an offence against the dignity of the law."

"If slaves were taught to read the Bible, why, then, they could read other books, too, and you know that wouldn't do. Everybody can see that it is dangerous to enlighten slaves."

"Ah; yet you are going round begging money to enlighten the far-off heathen. 'Oh, consistency, thou art a jewel!'"

"I haven't come for argument, but for help in

the cause of sending the Bible to the destitute, and the gospel to the heathen."

" I will no more be guilty of the inconsistency of putting money for such a purpose into the hands of men whose acts give the lie to their professions. In your missionary speeches you tell us of the degraded condition of the heathen ; you talk of the polygamy and other vices practised amongst them ; you mention their wars, their barbarity, and their ignorance; and from this state of depravity you propose to redeem them if we will but furnish the funds. How can we believe you sincere in your professions of pity for the heathen you have never seen, when there are four millions of benighted beings in your own country no less degraded, for whom you manifest no concern ? Worse than that : from these four millions you are careful to withhold the means and opportunity of enlightenment and elevation. And how much worse is polygamy than a certain vice which is common in this country, and which your slaves are encouraged if not compelled to practise ? And do you not teach and often force them to disregard their marriage vows ?"

"I am not here to discuss subjects of that sort."

"If you are laboring to promote the cause of missions, you should by no means overlook the considerations to which I am calling your attention. To show the degraded condition of the heathen, you lay great stress on their habit of selling their captives taken in battle. Is it any better to sell persons who have never been at war with you? Regardless of parental and filial ties as well as of marriage vows, you sell parent or child, husband or wife, brother or sister, and even mothers from their tender babes; and not a few of you sell your own children when the mother happens to be a slave. Slave-holders do things that would bring a blush of shame to the cheek of a decent savage."

"Yes, yes; I see your drift. With half an eye, it's easy to see that you're an abolitionist."

"Call me what you choose; I will show you your inconsistency. Another thing: while you profess to be shocked at the warlike disposition of the heathen, you, as well as other pro-slavery preachers, urged the organization of the guer-

rilla bands, here in our midst, who are now robbing and murdering loyal citizens all over the
country."

"I hope they'll soon put a rope round your
neck, you Black Republican abolitionist." Saying which, Parson Longface made long strides toward the door, looking back as he went, evidently a little suspicious that Lioni's boot might
follow him.

"The borer got bored this time," remarked
Alonzo, as soon as the parson was out of hearing.

"Well, my dear boy, our lesson in astronomy
is not likely to amount to much, this morning."

"I must tell you a dream I had just before I
awoke this morning, Mr. Lioni, which seems to
have been caused by my looking at the stars so
long last night. Yet a part of the dream appears to have originated in the serious reflections I've lately had about the slaves my bachelor uncle willed me at his death. I've been
trying some time to persuade myself that it
would be no sin to sell them and put the money
in my pocket; yet I've had some scruples of
conscience about it."

"I'm in hopes then your dream had a wholesome moral to it."

"Methought that beautiful planet, Saturn, which you told me was a thousand times as large as the earth, came whirling through the vast regions of space toward our planet till it seemed to fill the whole heavens. You and I were together, looking alternately through the telescope at the great planet while it rapidly approximated our globe, and could distinctly see, not only towns and cities on its surface, but also their inhabitants. Near us stood father and mother, and my little sister and brother. The mulatto boy my uncle willed to me was also in the group. You said a collision of the two worlds was inevitable. Then methought we were greatly alarmed, and made sure doomsday had come. The thought of being crushed to atoms between two worlds petrified me almost; but you consoled us all by saying that such a death was to be coveted in preference to being butchered by the cut-throat guerrillas; and then you mentioned, as an additional consolation, that the wicked rebels would all be caught under the dead-fall."

"Ha! ha! I was vastly comforting in my suggestions."

"You had scarce done speaking, when the earth began to tremble; and the sun, which was almost down, suddenly rolled back up the heavens. 'Here we go,' said you; 'the earth has forsaken its orbit, and we are going in a straight line toward Saturn.' Directly, the sun disappeared; but, for the loss of his light, we were more than compensated by the splendor of Saturn's rings."

"I almost envy you the luxury of such a dream, Alonzo."

"Oh, but I was in the utmost terror all the while; yet the grandeur of the scene impressed me deeply. At last the collision came; but very unaccountably, and to our joyful surprise, the planets came softly in contact, almost without a jar. Methought the outer ring and tall mountains of Saturn prevented the bodies of the globes from coming in close contact."

"A very fortunate circumstance!"

"It gave me great relief, I assure you. Then, while we stood gazing and wondering, lo! a great air-ship, grandly constructed, and with wings as white as a swan's, and of vast dimensions, came gliding out from Saturn, and alighted close by where we were standing. To our still greater astonishment, a bevy of angelic-looking beings sallied forth from the aerial ship and surrounded us. They were so exceedingly beautiful, and arrayed in such splendid attire that we had no fear of them. While in ecstasies of admiration, and almost ready to worship the celestial beings, as they seemed, they all at once closed in and made us prisoners."

"Now you were in trouble again."

"Binding us with strong cords, they put us on board the ship and sailed off. By and by, we found ourselves in the midst of a splendid city, the like of which I had never before conceived. We were unbound, and brought out of the ship to be gazed upon by the inhabitants. What crowds gathered about us!—and oh, what beautiful women I saw! Their forms were elegant; features symmetrical and finely moulded; and oh, what complexions!—skin white as snow; lips ruby; eyes a clear sky-blue; cheeks damask and delicately tinted as the peach-blossom; and their apparel was of the most brilliant tissue. Both males and females appeared vastly superior to our race, not only physically, but likewise mentally. It took them but a few moments to comprehend and speak our language."

"You must have felt a spirit of adoration for such superior beings."

"Alas! all my enthusiasm over their angelic appearance soon oozed out at the ends of my fingers and toes; for it directly became evident that our kidnappers intended to sell us for slaves."

"Horrible!"

"Indeed, I've hardly recovered yet from the terrible sensations I had while standing on the block to be sold into perpetual slavery."

"Ho, ho! you now have some idea how a poor darky feels when he's snatched away from his native country and sold into hopeless bondage."

"One at a time we were compelled, methought, to stand on a block till knocked off to the highest bidder. The rascals felt of my muscles and examined my limbs to determine how much hard work I was able to endure. They opened my mouth, looked at my teeth, punched me in the ribs, pulled my ears, twitched my nose, and hit me with their canes to see how sprightly I could move round; and what a deal of fun they made over my clumsy gait and swarthy complexion! But I stood it all like a philosopher till they put my mother on the block and treated her in the same manner; then, methought, my blood boiled like lava in the heart of Vesuvius!"

"No wonder. Oh, what a fearful dream you had! And how thankful you felt, when on waking you found it but a dream! But how many poor black men have passed through similar scenes,— and that without the joy of waking to find it all a dream."

"'Have you no regard,' said I, 'for the principles of justice? We have wronged you not; how can you thus deprive us of liberty and make us your slaves? Surely your hearts are not made of stone; you will yet be moved by a touch of pity, if not a sense of justice, and set us at liberty. Oh, ye noble sons of Saturn, it is impossible you should delight in oppression and remorselessly trample on our rights to liberty and the pursuit of happiness.' 'Men of your complexion,' replied he, 'have no rights which the fair-skinned inhabitants of Saturn are bound to respect. Instead of complaining of your lot, you ought to be profoundly thankful for having been brought from the dark, degraded condition, and the miserable world in which you were born, to such a sphere as this. Your race is always at war, and take a diabolical delight in tormenting, butchering, and devouring one another. Besides, your natural inferiority gives us the undoubted right to make slaves of you. This yellow man by your side was a slave to you until you yourself became a slave. Is he further below you than you are below me? The difference between your color and his is very slight, while the contrast between my complexion and yours is very great. If you had the right to make a slave of him on the ground of color, or upon the plea of inferiority of form or feature, or of intellect, then, on any or all of these grounds I have the right to make a slave of you.'"

"He rather had you there, Alonzo. How did you reply to that?"

"Said I, 'He was not kidnapped as I have been.' 'Ah, but his ancestors were,' replied he; 'your descendants, too, will be slaves without having . been kidnapped. If his ancestors were wrongly enslaved, then has he been wrongly enslaved.' 'But I had nothing to do,' said I, 'in first introducing slavery.' 'Neither had I,' returned he; 'the kidnappers brought you here, and I've paid my money for you; so you see nothing can be more plain than that I am your rightful owner, and that you are justly my property.'"

"There he had you again. And how did you get round that?"

"My conscience so condemned me, I could make no answer; but only begged that, though doomed to hopeless servitude, we might not be separated so as to be entirely deprived of each other's society."

"And what said he, then?"

"'The interests of the master,' he coolly responded, 'and not of the slave, must be consulted as to that.' And there I was confounded again; for I remembered that was my father's creed, and the doctrine of slave-holders gener-ally. I, too, had imbibed the same sentiment to some extent. How I wondered that I never be-fore had seen the palpable injustice of it."

"Ah, it was then brought home to you, and you saw it in a new light. How difficult it is for us to learn that Christian precept of doing unto others as we'd have them do unto us."

"Methought our masters allowed us a few mo-ments only to embrace and take final leave of one another. The parting scene threw me into such an agony of mind I instantly awoke."

At this moment a neighbor came running in to tell the terrible news of the massacre at Law-rence ; whereupon Lioni and Alonzo rushed out upon the street where a crowd was gathering round a few of the returned banditti. Dr. Puff and Skedaddle mixed in the throng, and were jubilant over the burning of Lawrence and the murder of the inhabitants. The cut-throats be-gan to express some fear of being pursued by Jim Lane, and the possibility that their com-panions, who lingered behind, had been over-taken by the avengers of blood. At this juncture the stragglers, of whom they were just speaking, came into town under whip and spur, with a detachment of Lane's men led by Knickerbocker, hard after them.

"Remarkable!" cried Skedaddle, and, wheeling about, trusted once more to his legs. Dr. Puff, no less terrified, followed in his wake; but, having more beef to carry, failed to keep up with the slim-shanked, lean-ribbed Skedaddle. They fled in the same direction with the flying banditti. The Union troops loaded and fired as they went, bringing down two or three of the cutthroats every round. Overtaking Dr. Puff, Knickerbocker couldn't resist the temptation of sticking his bayonet in his back for old acquaintance' sake. The Dr. bellowed lustily, but on rode Knickerbocker, still pursuing and shooting at the banditti. A few jumps brought him alongside the other excited nabob; of course, he felt in duty bound to pay his respects to him, also; a quick and vigorous thrust with the bayonet cut short the half-uttered "Remarkable!"

Knickerbocker is confident there are two traitors less in Platte County besides the thinning out of the cut-throats, in which he and his detachment did a thriving business the day after the Lawrence massacre.

"Alonzo, my brain is on fire!" said Lioni; "my blood is boiling in my veins! The thought — oh, the terrible thought — of that massacre at Lawrence!"

"I hope these soldiers will get the last one of the fiends that did it," responded the lad.

"But Missouri is full of just such men, if men they may be called. My mind is now made up to join the army, and, if need be, spill my last drop of blood in defence of the Union, and in sweeping from the face of the earth these lawless desperadoes. And I will go at once."

"So soon?"

"Yes; right away. Alonzo, I may see you no more! — God bless you! — Farewell! Let your aim be high, your purpose noble; live for heaven, for your country, and for humanity.

"Remember, —

' We live in deeds, not years, — in thoughts, not breaths;
In feelings, — not in figures on a dial.
We should count time by heart-throbs. He most lives
Who thinks most, feels the noblest, acts the best.' "